T0146828

It's Always Sunrise Somewhere
and Other Stories

From the Acclaimed Author of
"Sparks in the Dark"

Jacques Fleury

authorHOUSE®

AuthorHouse™
1663 Liberty Drive
Bloomington, IN 47403
www.authorhouse.com
Phone: 1 (800) 839-8640

Photo of Jacques Fleury by Jon Heinrich

Published by AuthorHouse 08/09/2016

ISBN: 978-1-5246-1518-5 (sc)
ISBN: 978-1-5246-1517-8 (e)

Library of Congress Control Number: 2016910159

Print information available on the last page.

Any people depicted in stock imagery provided by Thinkstock are models, and such images are being used for illustrative purposes only. Certain stock imagery © Thinkstock.

This book is printed on acid-free paper.

For my mother Marie Evelyne Toussaint:
My Hope & Inspiration
For my father Andre Fleury: My Levity & Eternal Adoration
For my sister Valerie K. Bouquet: My Respect & Fascination
For my nieces Nata & Nyny: My Joy & Liberation

Foreword

I am a Storyteller. I capitalize the "S" to bring emphasis to this art as a profession, although to most it provides no empirical means of sustainable income, unless you're Stephen King or someone equally as "lucky." Yet still, I am, among other things, a Storyteller, even though in my heart I know that the truth of who we are is not "I am this" or "I am that" but "I am." An earnest bit of wisdom I have learned as a truth seeker while on my spiritual journey studying Eckhart Tolle's "A New Earth: Awakening to Your Life's Purpose" and Raja Yoga Mindfulness Meditation. But for this purpose, I am a Storyteller. A Storyteller tells stories, thus prepare to be taken on a narrative journey; where the prima facie impossible becomes plausible, where hate becomes love and love becomes hate, where beasts morph into beauty and beauty morphs into beasts; where lines are drawn in the battle of man versus nature and nature versus man; culminating to our ultimate purpose: a yearning for human kindness in an ever elusive utopian world. Read these myriad stories, these mercurial, precarious and sometimes gregarious offerings of human fragility and fraternity, stories that transcend racial and class barriers in an effort to manifest the unity and commonality of the human experience.

Jacques Fleury, 2016

"It's always sunrise somewhere; the dew is never all dried at once; a shower is forever falling; vapor is ever rising. Eternal sunrise, eternal sunset, eternal dawn and gloaming, on sea and continents and islands, each in its turn, as the round earth rolls." John Muir

Contents

3 a.m. at The Café

It sits on a quaint yet poorly lit country road right alongside a towering willow tree that casts a sinister shadow over it. It is painted light blue with white trimmings with low windows and upon closer inspection, the paint has started to come off. The café itself is also dimly lit with light fixtures that hang low on the tables and booths. On the walls, there is an array of autographed pictures of somewhat famous people who's been there; all of them in black and white. A country singer is singing on the radio about love and lost. Behind the counter is a middle aged waitress with her hair up in a beehive as if she stepped right out of a photograph of a 1950's drive-in movie lot. She is chewing on a piece of gum and contouring her nails. Suddenly, the bell on the door chimes and the waitress glances up. "Hi there Billy Bob, it's about time someone showed up. I've been bored ta tears in this place. Ya'll have ya usual?" She asks raising her eyebrows while grinning, her gum is visible when she speaks. "Ya know it," he responds as he climbs on the center stool while taking off his cowboy hat and gloves.

"So, how's the truckin' business? Pick up any weirdo's on the road lately?" She asks from the open window in the kitchen as she prepares his food.

"As a matter of fact, jest yestiday I picked up this fella who said he waz headin' ta Mexico and said he waz willin' ta go as far as I would take 'em and since I waz headin' that way anyways, I told 'em ta hop on in. So we started talkin' and I asked 'em why waz he goin' ta Mexico? Cause ya know people on the run always seem ta go ta Mexico. And befo' I knew it, the bastard pulled a gun out on me and told me ta shut up and drive. So I ended up drivin' him ta the freakin' Mexican borda and then he told me ta forget that I ever saw 'em befo' he leaped off the truck and disappeared inta the woods."

"My goodness, ya jest never know who ya gonna run inta drivin' that truck of yers, huh?" She says as she places his food and coffee in front of him. "Yeah, aint that right," Harry says as he casually sips his coffee.

The door goes *cling, cling, cling* announcing a couple. The man has a goatee, is tall with a muscular build and broad shoulders and his face is blank as he holds the door for the woman to come in. Her shoulders are stooped forward with her head down. The man gets to a table and pulls her chair, he pauses and looks down at her for about five seconds and sighs before he sits down. "Matilda, can we get a menu," he says with partial amusement in his voice knowing that Matilda already knows what they want. Matilda smiles, puts her hands on her hips and says, "Don't start with me Jimmy Dean...always sucha smart ass," before heading to the kitchen. Jimmy Dean stares at his companion sitting across from him. She alternates between looking up at him and down at the table like a shy child. Sometimes she would open her mouth to speak, then changes her mind and closes it right back up again.

"I think its best. Ya'll see, it won't hurt a bit. I know plenty of weeman who done it and they all says it's a cinch. Ya in and ya out, jest like that," Jimmy Dean says with his hands over hers all the while stroking it with his thumb. "Jest like that, it won't hurt a bit." She looks at him briefly and puts her head down again as she begins to cry silently; her hand placed tightly over her mouth. The window where they sit now bears a luminescent glow as the moon creeps from behind a mass of clouds to light up the dimly lit surroundings. "Don't cry...Ya know I don't like ta see weeman cry, it jest breaks ma heart, honey please. Trust me, it's fo' the best." As he wipes her tears, she stares at the wedding ring on his finger and she cries even harder; her shoulders heaving up and down. Just then, Matilda brings them their food. "Hey, what's goin' on here? What's wrong darlin'? Ya look like ya jest lost a child..." She says as she tilts her head trying to make eye contact with the woman. "It's nothin'," Jimmy Dean answers, "its jest her hormones playin' tricks on 'er," he says as he taps her right hand half smiling.

Cling, cling, cling... and in walks two men with matching plaid shirts and salt and pepper hair. They take slow heavy steps to way at the other end of the café. Matilda walks over as she takes her pen and pad from her apron, still chewing on the same piece of stale gum. "Well howdy strangers, I haven't seen you two boys fo' a while now, "she says with a sparkly and knowing grin. I'll bring yall ya usual." Just as Matilda is getting ready to walk away, the man closest to her grabs her arm. "I know that we usually get the fish, but this time we both in the mood fo' a juicy steak, so it raises our blood pressure, at least we'll both die happy, eh?" Matilda lets out a hearty laugh as she walks away and says inaudibly, "It must be the full moon."

"Did you and Ann Marie have a talk?"

"Yes, last night."

"How did she take it?"

"Not well. Twenty years down the drain. I feel jest terrible."

"Well, don't. It is what it is...Mary Ann balled her eyes out when I told 'er. She acted like she never saw it comin', which I think it's a bunch of bull. She always had to chase me fo' sex. I never once went after her."

"Well, Ann Marie is ya typical dumb blond. She found a Hunks of the Midwest calendar unda ma bed and asked me why I didn't jest hang it up instead of keepin' it unda the bed. Unbelievable!" Just then, Matilda brings the men their order. They make eye contact as she grins and winks at them before leaving. "Remember the time when we were watchin' the game while she waz workin' the late shift at the Wal-Mart and she came home ta find me sleepin' with ma head on yer lap? Well she thought that that waz 'jest the sweetest thing she ever did see....',"he says in a high pitched voice in an attempt to mimic Ann Marie's. "She's as dumb as a bag of hammers that one."

"Well, at least now the cat is out of the bag."

"I don't care anymore. If people wanna talk, let 'em talk. Fuck 'em all!"

"Yeah, fuck 'em all!"

Cling, cling, cling... a woman and a man walk in. She is wearing white pumps, a tight short red dress, her breasts practically heaving over it, heavy make-up, big round white earrings, a string of clinging bracelets in her right arm and bright red lipstick while pulverizing a piece of gum which is visible when she talks. The man is dressed in a brown suit and yellow tie. He is looking around the room and over his shoulders as he approaches a booth the furthest away from everybody else as possible. They both slide in before Matilda struts over with pad and pen at the ready. The man just requests glasses of water for them both while they pretend to peruse the menu.

"So, how much?" Asks the man.

"Depends on what ya want," says the woman as she pops her gum.

"Well, I've never done this before and to be honest, I'm a little nervous."

"Don't be honey...I won't bite...unless ya want me ta...but that'll cost ya extra...," she tilts back her head and laughs. When she realizes that he is taking her seriously she reassures him, "Relax honey...I'm jest kiddin'. Ya so seeerious, loosen up a bit... ya married types kill me!"

The man leans forward and whispers, "I just want to go to a motel and just talk at first,"

"Talk?! Well, it's ya money honey...lets go then," She says as they both get up to leave.

They are the last customers to leave The Café. As Matilda tends to the task of cleaning up, she stops, walks over to open a window and sticks her head out. She closes her eyes; which are tilted towards the sky and with a closed mouthed grin she inhales—holds it for a few seconds—and exhales. Outside the birds are chirping and the sun slithers from below the earth to greet the dawning of a new day.

Faded Blue Jeans

I love goatees. Maybe I wasn't really in love with him; just his goatee. Shallow, huh? Well you don't understand this goatee was unique. Unique because it belonged in the goatee hall of fame. The smile behind it wasn't too bad either. Hank was his name. I used to see him around school when I went to college in Andover, Indiana. Good old Indiana State. He used to walk around with a couple of books firmly planted against his sturdy hips, with a disarming smile displaying his pearly whites. He would often wear slightly snug fading blue jeans with a "Dead Can Dance" T-shirt neatly tucked in. Occasionally, he'd notice me gawking and he'd wink and give me a coy smile, like I was one of his buddies or something. It was during these moments that I started planning my next move.

One day, I was out strolling downtown Handover and came upon Bacords Book Store. It was this little off beat store consisting of new and old books and whatever baked goods the local housewives would bring in to sell to the owners, Glitch and Stitch. Yes, I know. Remember, this is Indiana territory here. As I look through the display window outside the store, I saw this book with bright green cover and bold white letters that read "How to Get the School Hunk." That's when I knew that the spirits were on my side that day, that hour, that minute! So, of course I went in to check it out. "How ya doin' Sam?" Stitch usually greets me first followed by Glitch.

"What ya up to Sam?" They ask simultaneously.

"Oh, ya know, this and that," I said barely audible and scurry away as to avoid any more nagging questions from the pesky, but oh, so handsome twins. Rumors are that they are actually lovers, but it's all kept very hush hush. But back to Mission Hank Possible.

I went over to the relationship section and grabbed the book so hard that my fingers almost made dent marks on the cover. I opened and skimmed it. I find that it helps me cut through the crap. For example instead of reading a chapter entitled "So you like Hank", I want to go straight to the chapter entitled "How to get Hank to play naked twister!" So, after scanning the contents, I started to flip through the pages for the chapter entitled, "Find out what you have in common and use it to move beyond the 'Hi' and 'Bye' phase." Got it! We're both student tutors! As I think about this, Chellby Lynn is playing on the radio. I went to "Now that you've found something in common, learn how to talk to him without drooling." After ringing up my purchase, Stitch and Glitch gave each other knowing looks as I dashed out of there with a knowing smirk.

I stumbled onto him around the tutoring area the next day. "Hi Hank!" You a tutor?" Duhhh… Like I didn't know.

"Looks like it." He was smirking as he said this. "Don't you write for the school paper?"

"Yeah… How did you know?"

"I read your article on the importance of diversity and tolorance on college campuses. So I asked my friend Jeff who you are. He writes the sports column"

"Yeah…right", I trailed my words, flabbergasted that he knew so much about me already! My heart started racing, like a child fearing his parents are on the brink of discovering his secret. I wondered what else he knew about me. Did he know that I get a mushrooming stiffy every time I watched him walk down the hallway? His coconut shaped buttocks toying with the rough fabric of his faded blue jeans, toying with my heart and both my heads if you know what I mean.

Calm down…don't blow this, I told myself. You should have seen him sitting there, with the chair turned backwards so that his chest and biceps, swollen with youth, rested against the back of the chair; his baseball cap on backwards and his usual attire of t-shirt and faded blue jeans.

"So what what do do you you tu…tutor?" I stuttered. *Don't blow it, well at least not yet.*

"Beginning French, you?" I could not believe my ears, you know like hearing your name called out as a prize winner and staring at your ticket in disbelief. I speak French! You see, French is Haiti's national language.

"What a coincidence!" I beamed. "I speak French…, although not as well as I used to. But it's part of my native tongue!" My chest was heaving ferociously. I kept hoping that he wouldn't notice the sorry state he'd put me in.

"Well, that's awesome senator! Maybe you can tutor me!" He was half laughing by this time.

"Sure, why not." I failed miserably at being nonchalant. "I tutor English composition by the way."

"Great! I'll definitely need your help with structuring my papers. When I write, I'm all over the place." He joked.

"Sure…" I tried not to drool.

"Well, my appointment is here, gonna get to work." He is all that and diligent too?!

"Yeah, sure… Say why don't I give you my number, maybe we can go for a wine cooler or something." Wine cooler? But the words seem to jump out of my mouth like coach roaches that have fortuitously fallen on hot grease!

"Sure, senator, why not." I wondered why he called me senator. I wasn't on student government. But who cares, it sounded hip, cool and sooo masculine! I wrote my number on the front cover of his notebook, after dismissing the idea to write it on his bicep that seem to do its own backward forward dance as he extends his vein filled forearms to bid me goodbye.

As I skipped down the empty hallway towards the exit, I couldn't help but feel giddy about the fact that I just made a possible date with Hank Zozoni! I felt like Little Red Riding Hood skipping her merry way on the way to Grandma's house. Hopefully Hank would be the big bad wolf who provides me with a much needed distraction from sexual frustration. As I thought about this, my cock stood at attention. I opened the double doors and greeted the winter air, and strutted over the hardened ice with the flare of a sophomore ice skater. I unlocked my bike and rushed home to lay dream like in bed and use the phone as my pillow, waiting wanting Hank to call.

When I got home, the house felt completely still. I came through the back door opening to the kitchen. I could hear the grandfather clock in the living room and the refrigerator's hum, threatening the silence. I grabbed a beer from the fridge and ran up the back staircase to my room. You know, to do stuff, things I normally would put off. Like homework, putting all my CDs in their *right* cases, read my mail and sort out my porn collection by level of performance and the star's sex appeal. And one more thing, live or die by the phone waiting for Hank's highly anticipated call.

As I anticipated Hank the Hunk to call, I heard the front door slammed shut. Mom and Dad were home. In that very moment, the phone rang. I pounced trying to get to it first.

"Allo," wanting to sound French just in case it's you know who.

"Hi! Is Sam there please?" Yessss! It's him!

"Who's calling please?" Like I didn't know.

"Hank Zozoni." He is very cool.

"Let me see if he's home." I hoped he didn't recognize my voice. I paused for dramatic effect. "Hey, Hank! What's up?" Mr. Nonchalance is my new name, as I raise my voice to sound more jovial than before, so Hank would know I was glad to hear from him.

"Hey Sam. Too soon to call?"

"Noooo!" I was hoping you would!" Hoping I didn't sound too needy.

Then he told me he needs help writing his newly assigned English paper.

"How about my place? We can study by the pool. My parents are flying to Bora Bora for the weekend."

"Well?" I was on the edge of my seat!

"Well what?" He sounded like he was in a stupor.

"You wanna come over?" I was hyperventilating.

"Oh, yeah sure. Why not? I'll bring my bathing suit," he said with a snort.

Hank showed up in a pair of dark blue sweat pants and a burgundy colored sweat shirt and his soccer jacket with his number on it, sixty six. In Haiti, the number 66 is a derogatory way of calling someone a faggot, "deux sis kole!" "two sixes together!" they'd shriek at you but Hank hadn't a clue and I didn't dare tell him. Its late fall and the air was becoming dense and chilly. It's a good thing we have both an outdoor and an indoor pool. We immediately head down to the pool and I started to look through Hank's first draft. I felt a sudden shadowy heat around me, and I looked up to see Hanks pearly whites hovering over my head, his face youthful and glowing. And I felt like I was basking in the sun.

"Whatttt?" I feigned annoyance.

"So, is it good?" I was glad that he wanted my approval.

"It's *ok*. Your grammar and punctuation are excellent as well as your use of transition words to keep your paragraphs connected, but there's no definite thesis statement and your thoughts are in disarray." I maintained a professional composure.

"My thoughts are in waaht?" He raised his nose as if he smelled something funny.

"In disarray, all over the place, with no clear direction..."

"Alright, alright...I get it." He acted exasperated. "I oughta kick yo ass for dissing my paper like dat."

And with that he lunged at me and dragged me into the pool with the paper still in my hand. I held the paper above my head so as not to get it wet as I climbed back out of the pool. I ran cautiously around the pool after him, my jeans, heavy as chlorinated fluid clang to my crotch exposing the beginnings of an erection. Hank stood on the other side, grinning, his legs twitching, knowing that I was coming. I started after him, but he jumped into the pool fully clothed before I even had a chance to get to him. I jumped in. He didn't know that I'm a better swimmer than he was. I caught up to him easy. I pounced onto his back. At that point we simultaneously toppled over and his weight almost drowned me. He wiggled under my grasp trying to get a way; I lowered my hands further down to his groin area, pleasantly surprised to see that he too was erect with the cataclysmic force of rushing adrenaline. Hank wiggled like a trapped snake. His masculine backside bumped against my pelvic, toying with my palpable stiffness. I gasped fearing my own desire, failing to realize that I have freed the thick white fluid that threatened to explode my gonads, sending spurts of joy all in the confines of my now severely tight blue jeans. I started to panic hoping that Hank wasn't aware of this. What if he turns around and upon seeing my conspicuous desire barks out "fag!!!" at me or something.

He twisted around in a half circle and pushed me away from him playfully. I landed on my back, my head partly sank below the surface and some water got into my nose. I came up gasping for air and wrapped my pleading arms around his lithe body. To my surprise he does the same and our crotches met and greeted one another with equal desire. He was still fully erect. At that point he was breathing heavier than I was, like a lion, having chased and caught his prey, panting to catch his breath before he devours it. He looked at me absorbedly. I knew he knew my soul and vice versa. We understood the satanic nature of forbidden desire. We also knew that it was only a matter of time before we succumbed to it. I wrapped my lips around his as tightly as the wrapper around a candy made sticky by excessive heat. He kissed me back ferociously. His lips took to mines as the parched Arizona desert takes to rainfall.

He kissed my eyes so that I could see better, my ears so that I could hear clearer and finally my head, so that it could all finally come together. We got out of the pool and eagerly consummated our passions in my bedroom.

The next day I was fidgeting for something in my locker. It was late and the college was somber. Most of the students that live there went home for the weekend or out to the bars given that it was a Friday night. I heard footsteps coming down the hall, but I didn't see the bodies they were attached to. It's kind of like those horror flicks where the predictable plot is scarier than the movie; except I decided not to play the paralyzed victim waiting to meet my regrettable fate. I closed my locker and made a run for it! I didn't look back, like those fearful victims in those types of movies. But it was no use. My fate was set.

I came face to face with a group of jocks from the soccer team. They stood there, their arms crossed, their smirks perfectly in place. As I became aware of what was about to happen to me, something in my mind must have shut down. It must have been a visceral reaction of the fight or flight response of my central nervous system, because the last thing I remember before I blanked out and the blows started coming like a basketball to a worn out hoop, was Hank's face. He stood there, the epitome of cool, arms crossed, lips in a distorted snarl, rocking slowly back and forth and looking at me like someone watching a pile of dog shit being discarded off.

***

Hank graduated and moved away shortly thereafter. I heard that he got married and doing the suburban family thing somewhere in Arizona. I never knew exactly why things happen the way they did. However, I did not let it destroy me. My name is still Sam Toujour. Sure, I went on to have a few equally explosive and poisonous relationships, but I'd like to call those times my "guess 'n test" phase. I decided that the best thing to do is to get to know myself for a while. Maybe eventually learn why I attract fuck ups in my life. What is it about me that draw them to me like flies? You know the saying "you can catch more flies with honey than you can with vinegar". Well, I don't want to catch any flies at all.

A Place Where Love Lives

Morning has broken. I am rising in perfect synchronicity with the sun and I am glad to be glad. I can see it just by lifting my head over my pillow to peak at the window just above my bed. It's 5:45 a.m. I will be up in another 15 minutes. But meanwhile, I'm just enjoying staring at the sun.

I am now kneeling in front of the window, my hands neatly interwoven on the windowpane underneath my chin. Right now, right here, I am happy. The day holds limitless potential, a Tabular Rasa (a blank slate) as the philosopher John Locke puts it. I'm thinking about how great it will feel to turn sixteen exactly one week from today, Sunday March 15th, 1987,The Ides of March as written in the Shakespearian play "Julius Caesar"; inferring that something eventful will happen that day. I decide to turn on my clock radio and just my luck; one of my favorite songs is playing. "Enjoy the Silence" by Depeche Modes. I have it on low just enough so that I can also hear the sound of the morning rustling its leafy feathers like a young bird waking under the warm wings of its mother. The sun is rising out of the belly of the Smokey North Carolina Mountains. Its color is reddish orange and I could feel its warmth, like lingering fingers caressing my cheeks and I cannot help but smile. Daddy John and Pappi Jake are still in bed. Yeah, that's right, I have two dads. You are probably wondering why.

Well, the story goes like this. I'll tell it to you as it was told to me. My mother was only 17 years old by the time I was a 1 year old baby. She crumbled under the pressure to raise a child as an unwed mother in a fairly small conservative town of Happersville, North Carolina. My biological father, Daddy John, was eighteen however and my mom Emilou and her mom and dad decided that maybe it would be best if dad raised me since he was already out of high school and earning a living pumping gas at the local gas station. Mom went back to finish high school and would visit me on the weekends. I remember vaguely the excitement I used to feel when dad told me that today was a "mommy day." Dad told me I would jump up and down clapping my hands clumsily and yelling "Yeh, Yeh, mommy mommy" grinning with my sparse teeth. By the time I was three years old, mom finished high school and desperately wanted to go away to college because she felt "stifled" in Happersville and wanted more for herself than most of the girls in town who simply wanted to become housewives and spend the rest of their lives cooking, cleaning and gossiping with each other on the front porch. So Emilou, left to pursue loftier dreams like pursuing a degree in theatre and acting at New York University and dad stayed behind to take care of me. God bless him. I would see mom about three times a year for the next ten or so years, birthdays, Christmas and Thanksgiving. And then the visits dwindled as the years went on until she stopped visiting all together and would only call and send the occasional card in the mail.

Dad eventually went to trade school to become a mechanic. We continued to live in Happersville but dad moved to a two-bedroom apartment when I got to be too old to sleep in the same bed as him. I used to love cuddling up to dad in bed, his big arms wrapped firmly around my small frame, offering me security in an insecure world. Every night at bedtime, he would tell me bedtime stories and kiss me on my cheek never failing to say "Daddy loves you" and I would smile and respond, "Andy loves daddy too." He never got another girlfriend after Emilou left and only his male buddies would come over our place to watch the World Wrestling Federation. But he never brought anyone home to spend the night, that is, until he met daddy Jake.

I remember one day, during one of daddy Jake's visits, I came out of my room to go use the bathroom. The TV was showing snow and making some type of white noise and the lights were off. As I got closer to the couch, I saw daddy John laying with his head on daddy Jake's chest with their hands wrapped around each other. I wasn't shocked or disgusted at all like some of my friends would be. I thought it was the most natural thing in the world. I felt relieved that dad finally had someone stay overnight. The next morning, I found them in the kitchen together. Dad was making breakfast looking back and smiling occasionally at daddy Jake and daddy Jake was just staring at him giggling and smiling back like an overjoyed teenager. And I remember thinking; I don't ever want this moment to end. I don't ever want daddy Jake to leave. And he didn't. He moved in soon after and we've been happy together ever since.

Now it's just about six o'clock and the birds are chirping noisily in our garden. My dads are probably going to sleep in today as usual and get up just in time for brunch. They both love a good brunch. They say that all gay men do. And I'm still not sure why I'm up so early on a Sunday morning. Then I gleefully remember! I want to catch the 8 a.m. service at St. Mary's Church located in downtown Happersville. I've been going to this Church for the last 5 weeks without my dad's knowledge. You see, there are a few things about me they don't know: that I'm Christian and that I'm gay. I'm almost positive they won't have a problem with the latter. However, being that they are both Agnostic, I'm not sure how they will react to my Christian beliefs. I have heard them talk in not so complimentary ways about the Catholic Church, about how "they" reject gays even while they are committing homosexual acts themselves with the altar boys that serve under them. How hypocritical they are about professing "Christian values" and perpetuating unholy acts against the very people they're supposed to protect. So no, I haven't told them about my being Christian. But I must confess, there is another reason as to why I've started going to St. Mary's. The reason is a tall, beefy blond haired blue eyed, hunk of practical fantasy named Billy and believe you me honey, he's is more than plenty for this old boy. The scandalous thing about all this is he happens to be the Priest's son (he had him *before* he decided to become a Priest) and I'm not even sure if he's gay and even if he is, I wouldn't be surprised if he decides to stay in the closet for years given his father's position in this small community. But he works as one of the altar boys and our eyes have met numerous times and he always gives me an inviting smile. But I usually leave right after the service instead of hanging around for coffee hour so that I could get the scoop on him. But today is going to be different. Today, I will be brave and boldly stay for coffee hour and actually have a conversation with "holy boy" and confront my worst fear: that he is straight or not interested. Or it could turn out that he is in fact a flaming fag and we end up living happily ever after like my dads.

So after I shower and get dressed, I gobbled down a glass of carnation instant breakfast and head straight for the door. When I step outside into the blossoming morning, I spread my arms wide open to greet God, much like the flowers spread their petals to greet the sun. I linger on the front steps just long enough to inhale the air and feel the breeze slowly penetrate my entire body and it feels like mother nature has just revived me by administering cardiopulmonary resuscitation (CPR) and I become bloated with life ready to take on anything that comes my way. I go to the garage, get my bike and ride it into town pedaling it as if I was already late when in fact I have a whole hour to get to the Church that is only half an hour away. As I pedaled down the road, I look around me at all the things I usually take for granted. The horses, cows and farm animals on my neighbors farms; old cars parked in weed ridden driveways, my neighbors already up and sitting on their front porches waving hello as I pass by. Most of them have known me all my life and I take comfort in that.

When I get into town, I notice that some of the older members are already making their way into the Church to have their usual alone time before the service starts. I decide to rest my bike against this weeping willow tree and sit down with my legs folded under me to wait until Father William Bogan and his son Billy arrive.

After the Church service ended, I figure it's now or never to finally pounce on Billy Bogan Jr., the Church's holy hunk. "Missing you" by John Waite plays in my head. I take a quick look around the room and notice Billy talking to one of the silly giggly girls who fawn all over him while he does his best to look like he's listening to their school girl gibberish. I walk over to the table with the treats and help myself to some tea and a corn muffin when suddenly I hear this thunderous yet calm voice behind me, "Hey, is your name Todd Jenkins?" I look over my shoulders to see Billy towering over me. "Jack and Diane" by John Melloncamp, plays in my head. He seems much bigger up close. He has a square jarred face structure, shortly cropped blond hair that flutters over his forehead, sky blue eyes and perfectly straight white teeth and clean-shaven. "Chameleon" by Boy George plays in my head. He is wearing a white shirt, a yellow tie with a yellow sweater over it and corduroy pants. He is spotless. He is beautiful.

"Why yes, I am. And you must be William Bogan Jr." I say as I extend my hands to him. "I'm Your Venus" by Bananarama plays in my head. He grabs my hand almost too quickly and squeezed it firmly and I am too taken aback to squeeze back. I am a little annoyed at myself because I do not want him to think that I'm one of those limp wristed insecure fags, which in reality, I sort of am.

"Nice to meetcha. I've always wanted to make you...urr...make your acquaintance I mean, but you always seem to take off right after the service," he says smilingly.

"Yeah, I guess I'm kinda shy that way," I reply with a ridiculously wide smile.

"So, you leave nearby?" He asks with a hopeful look on his face. "Do you really want to hurt me" by Boy George plays in my head.

"Yeah, just a thirty minute bike ride from here. And—and you?" I ask hesitantly.

"Yeah, Just a ten minute car ride from here." He says with a chuckle, after which there was an uncomfortable silence as we both avoid looking each other by looking around the room instead.

"Well, I guess I must be going. My dads will be wondering where I am." As soon as I spoke those words, I wanted to take them back knowing their inevitable implications.

"Your dads?" Here it comes. "What do you mean Dads? You have more than one?" He asks with his face attired in total puzzlement.

"Well, yeah. It's a long story. I'll tell you sometime. But I really must be going." As I make my way to the basement exit, Billy calls out "Wait! Can—can I call you sometime?" He asks hurriedly.

"Sure." I say as I quicken my steps.

"Well, aren't you forgetting something? What's your phone number?"

"Oh, yeah. Sorry." I write my number on the Church program and hand it to him from a distance, one foot in and one foot out the door so not to encourage any further small talk which might reveal more than I care to right then. At that point, I think I've talked plenty. "Toy soldiers" by Martica plays in my head.

"Thanks and nice chattin' withcha!" I hear him say as the basement door slams behind me. Outside, I feel a sense of great relief that I did it! I finally talked to Billy Bogan Jr., the man I'm destined to marry—that is, if he ever calls me. I get on my bike and ride home grinning with the mid morning sun napping on my back.

When I get home, I can tell that my dads are up because Liberace is playing in the living room and the smell of eggs and burnt toast is coming from the kitchen. For some reason that I care to know about, they only play Liberace on Sundays. Daddy John loves to cook, but he's not very good at it. And Daddy Jake loves him too much to complain about it, so he eats whatever his beloved dishes out.

"Todd? Is that you?" Daddy John yells from the kitchen.

"Uh...Yeah! Who else has a key to this house besides us three! Unless you have one more under the front door rug, conveniently placed for the occasional burglar that I don't know about!" I say with a smirk as I walk towards him and my legs strain to meet his taller frame to give him a kiss on his left cheek. I then start uncovering the pots on the stove.

"Do you always have to be such a smart ass? And leave those pots alone and go greet Daddy Jake before you hurt his feelings." He says as he slaps me on the butt. I walk over to my other dad and kiss him the same way. "Hello there handsome. What you've been up to these past few Sundays. You always seem to be up and about before we even get up?" Daddy Jake asks with eyes that swirl with curiosity and bemusement. "Time after time" by Cindy Lauper plays in my head.

"Uh..well. I've been going to St. Mary's for the early morning service." Just as I say that, I grab a piece of sausage patty and started to make my way up to my room when I hear: "Hold it right there Todd Jenkins!" Screams Daddy John. I can tell that I am in trouble. He always uses my full name when he's cross with me. "We are the world" by a bunch of Diva artists like Michael Jackson, Bruce Springsteern, Cindy Lauper and U2 plays in my head. "What's this Church business? Since when did you go to Church? You know how we feel about the Catholic Church?" I thought I noticed vapor coming out of his nostrils.

"Well, dad, I—I know how you feel, but you've always taught me to think for myself sooo...I believe in Jesus Christ. I'm a Christian dad. I'm sorry if that hurts your feelings, I certainly didn't..."

"Well, of course you should think for yourself. I'm just a little surprised is all. I just never saw it coming. Did you daddy?" He affectionately calls Daddy Jake "daddy", particularly because he's five years older and frankly is also the dominant one in the relationship if you get my drift.

"No. I never saw it coming either. But Johnny honey, we have raised him to think for himself sooo...we must support him and his beliefs, no matter how unbelievably wrong we think those beliefs are." He says while his eyebrows conjoined tightly together signifying how pissed off *he* really is. "What's Love Got To Do With It" by Tina Tuner plays in my head

"You know Todd, this makes me think about what else you've been keeping from us?" He asks with his right hand curved on his right hip a la teapot fashion and the other hand on the kitchen counter.

"Yeah, anything else you want to shock us with before we eat so that we won't choke on our brunch young man?" Asks Daddy Jake, still fuming.

"No. Not that I can think of...I gonna go. See you guys later." And with that, I galloped to my bedroom to wait by the phone for Billy Bogan Jr. to call. I sit on my bed with my guitar waiting with the phone inches away on the bed beside me. Pathetic, right? Oh, well. I really believe that he could be like my Daddy Jake is to Daddy John: he could be the one to make my life complete. I often daydream about us walking down the isle of St. Mary's hand in hand in our white tuxes on our way to get married by his Priest father no less. But, as my dads often remind me, my thoughts are often a little grandiose.

Just when I start strumming "While Horses", by the Stones on my guitar, the phone rings. I quickly throw my guitar on the bed, and leap on the phone like a Bear on a salmon. "Hello?" I say breathlessly.

"Hello. Is Billy there?" Just as I was about to answer, I heard Daddy John on the other phone. "Hello? Hello?"

"Its for me dad," I holler not hiding my annoyance. If it were for him, I would have announced it already. "Sorry." He says and hangs up.

"Hey, Billy." I say beaming from ear to ear.

"How did you know it was me?" *Because there's no other man in my life of whom I hope to marry except you.*

"I just knew." I try to play it cool.

"I really enjoyed talking to you at Church today."

"Yeah. I really enjoyed it too."

"Well, are you gonna tell me or not?"

"Tell you what?"

"About your two dads silly!"

"Oh yeah, that."

"Yeah. Spill it!"

"Well, my father is …well…gay and has a boyfriend or husband. Whatever you wanna call it." I held my breath and waited for the backlash. But none was forthcoming.

"Yeah? I think that's... interesting…"

"Interesting?"

"Yeah."

"How so?"

"Well, you have to admit, that's not too common around here."

"Yeah, you right about that. Are you freaked out by it?"

"Well, noooo....just a little surprised maybe. I know that my dad wouldn't approve being a Priest and all, but then again that's just him."

"So you ok with it?"

"Sure, why not? Em...does that mean...errrr....are you....I mean..."

"If you wanna know if I'm gay the answer is NO! Just because my dad is gay that doesn't mean that I..."

"Of course it doesn't. Sorry. I didn't mean to...just forget it ok?"

"Sure. Whatever." There was an uncomfortable silence.

"Billy, can I ask you something?"

"Sure."

"I've kinda noticed you looking and smiling at me during Church. Are you by any chance...g—"

"No way! How could you even think such a thing? My dad would kill me! I mean. Have you completely lost your mind?!"

"Sorry. Sorry. I didn't mean to upset you. It's just...well. Sorry, ok?"

"Sure. Whatever." Yet another period of uncomfortable silence.

"Billy?"

"Yeah?"

"What if I *was* gay. Would that freak you out?"

"No. Not really."

"Oh."

"What if *I* was. Would that freak *you* out?"

"No. 'Course not!" Silence.

"Todd, would you like to go biking together sometime?"

"Yeah, sure I would!" I say a little too eagerly. "I mean, that would be cool." I try to sound nonchalant.

"Great! How about tomorrow, after school? I go to the St. Mary's Catholic School. You know where that is?"

"Sure. It's the school right next to the baseball field. Would you like to meet at the field?"

"Sure. Say 3:30?"

"I'll be there." *Todd, brunch time!*

"My dad is calling me. See you tomorrow, k?" And hang up before giving him time to answer. My heart was beating almost as fast as a startled bird after talking to Billy. I worry that tonight I will not be able to sleep, tossing and turning with anticipation. The worst of it is, I glance down my pants and it seems that all the blood in my entire body has gone straight to my penis. So I wait a while before going downstairs knowing that that's one conversation I am not prepared to have with my dads.

I barely make it through school the next day. When the last bell of the day rings, I bolt for the door as if the school is on fire. I leap onto my bike and make my towards the baseball field. The early afternoon sun is bright with promise, as the wind gets playful with my shoulder length wavy brown hair. I am beaming with anticipation.

When I get there, I see no sign of Billy. My stomach tightens up with thoughts of the possibility of desertion. Have I been stood up? And so I wait. It was nearing four o'clock and I think common etiquette dictates that one should not wait more than twenty minutes for a date. Or is it thirty? Just as I am starting to go for my bike to head out, Billy comes running towards me. His silky blond hair lush and youthful in the late Spring air. He looks light and beautiful like a floating leaf.

"Hey there Todd. So sorry I'm late. One of my teachers wanted to talk to me after class" he says breathlessly yet smilingly.

"No prob. I knew you'd come." Which is somewhat true but not completely.

"So, where do you wanna go?" I ask.

"I don't know, anywhere I guess."

"Well, how about going to the nearby trail. It's pretty quiet and the scenery is simply fabuloussss!" The minute after I say fabulous especially with so much emphasis on the "s" I felt some regret because I thought it made me sound like a total queen and my fears are confirmed when Billy smirks and say "Fabulous?"

"Yeah, whatever. Let's just go."

When we get to the trail, at first we just stop and take in our earthly surroundings: he tall regal trees; the sound of the birds echoing like the voices of giddy children during recess; the smell of the bright green spring leaves. Neither one of us says anything for at least three minutes and then "You wanna race?" Billy asks.

"Sure why not." I say excitedly. Billy gets a head start. I start pedaling feverishly in hopes of impressing him with my athleticism. But I was no match for Billy, who, I found out later, is the star athlete of his swim team.

"Ok, ok, you win!" I say breathlessly.

"Ha ha! Now what should we do?" He asks grinning as a hint of sweat matted down his blond hair on his forehead.

"I know. What don't we play truth or dare?" I ask hesitantly.

"Truth or dare. I've never really liked that game."

"Uh, comonnnn…it'll be fun!" I say eagerly.

"For you maybe. What the heck, nothing else to do right?"

"Great. I'll go first. Truth or dare?" I ask him.

"Truth I guess." He says skeptically.

"When did you lose your virginity?" My heart starts to accelerate.

"What kind of question is that?"

"Oh come on Billy. You said you wou-"

"Alright alright," he cuts me off. "My virginity, hmmmm… that would be last year."

"With who?" I ask with pressing curiosity.

"I'd rather not say. Now my turn. Have you ever caught your dads having sex?" He asks with a smirk.

"Whaaaat? That's totally gross! What kind of q-"

"Uh uh uhhhh….you said-"

"Alright, alright you freak. I'll answer it. Yes I did. Once. It was around the time when they first started dating. They used to have sex a lot back then. I remember coming home from school and the house was unusually quite. So just as I started to go to my room upstairs I thought I heard some type of noise coming from my dad's bedroom. So I made my way there towards his door. And as I came closer, I heard some groaning and moaning and squeaking of the bed along with some mumblings that I could not quite make out what was being said. And then as I got closer I heard Daddy John say, "Oh yeah…give me that big…."

"Alright, alright…that's waaayyyy more than I needed to know," he interrupts by waving his hands in the air with raised eyebrows.

"My turn. Have you ever had a gay experience?" I could almost feel my heart readying itself to leap out of my chest.

"Oh so payback time, eh? As a matter of fact no. But I'm kind of curious about it. So there! Satisfied?" He asks widening his eyes.

"So. Ya curious, eh? What are you so curious about. I mean, what-what is it that you'd like to do *if* you were to have a gay experience." Boom boom! Boom boom! My heart cries out in excitement.

"Wouldn't you like to know?" He teases.

"Oh come on Billy! Be a sport!" I cry out in near desperation. "You either tell me or I'm gonna have to beat it out of you." I threaten as I start to get off my bike.

"Oh I'd like to see you try…" He says with a confident swagger. Just then, I start to make my way towards him, he dropped his bike and starts running. He is faster than me, in better shape than me so I try to run as fast as my short legs could take me. He is much taller than me. I'm 5 ft. 7 inches and he is six ft. one inches. I decide to hide behind one of the larger trees just to get him to stop running. He does. As I peak from behind the tree, I see him spinning around and wondering where I am.

"Hey Todd! Where you at?" I smile and say nothing trying to keep from laughing. "Tooooddd! Where the heck are ya?" He starts to make his way back towards me. As he draws nearer to where I am, I make a sudden move and leap from behind the tree and tackle him at waist level. He looses balance and falls to the ground. "You fucker! You gonna get it now!" He cries out as he tries to overpower me. In one sweeping move, he manages to flip me over so that he was now sitting on my crotch pinning me down with both hands on mines. "So, how long have you wanted to nail me?" I ask with a breathy grin.

"How long have you wanted to *be* nailed?" He huffs out as sweat drips down his forehead and onto my partially exposed belly. We just stared at each other while listening to one another's quickening breaths for about a minute. Then he suddenly drops on my chest and pressed his sweat smeared lips upon mines. He releases my hands to wrap it around my face and I use my newly freed hands and placed them on his buttocks gradually tightening them around his swimmers build derriere.

"Oh Todd! I want you so bad!" He says as he kisses my lips, nose, eyes, ears and occasionally licking my Adams apple and my the sweat streaming down my face with unabated hunger and shameless desire as I run my searching hands up and down his muscled back and broad shoulders. Our sex long and restless while bumping and grinding against each other. And to both our surprise, we let out this loud yelp as our sweaty soaked bodies swivel and swirls like a startled snake preparing for an attack while looking with both surprise and pleasure into each other's eyes. And Billy finally collapses on me with his head resting on my chest and I in return run my hands up and down his back slowly, tenderly but yet firmly. And we do this for about three minutes without saying anything because we feel that all that we needed to say has been said during our fervent physical and emotional encounter.

"Todd, I feel scared and happy at the same time. Is that weird?" I was glad that Billy spoke first.

"I feel the same way." I say with a resigned calmness in my voice.

"So, what-what are we gonna do?" He asks, almost sounding like a confused little boy and not the big senior stud that he is, at least to me. Now *I* feel in control, like I'm the bigger man now.

"Let's just take it one day at a time. We don't have to do or say anything right now. We'll go home and act like nothing special is going on. At least for now, k?"

"K." He looks at me with trust and tenderness. Shortly thereafter, we both get up and make our way home.

***

I don't see Billy until the following Sunday at church, the Ides of March has come. Today is March 15th and something horrific waits. I sit at my usual place near the front of the pulpit and wait while Billy does his best to avoid me. When the service is over, I go down to coffee hour hoping that we would get a chance to talk. When I get there, I see him listening and smiling while the usual bunch of silly giddy girls speed talks around him. I place myself in his direction so that he would notice me. He finally does briefly but quickly looks away. And just as I start to make my way towards him, he excuses himself and walks away out of the main room, down a corridor leading to the church office. I follow him with quick anxious steps. "Billy, wait…." I try to catch up to him. He goes into the office and just as he was about to close the door I push it open with my left hand. "We have to talk," I say.

"What about?" he asks with a nervous look on his face.

"Don't try to play dumb Billy, it doesn't suite you. About what happened in the woods remember?" I say with slight irritation in my voice.

"Oh, that." He says and looks away.

"Yeah, that." I look right into his eyes with quiet frustration and desperation.

"Well, what's to talk about? What happened happened." He says raising his hands in resignation.

"Yeah but, what does it mean?" I ask as my voice goes up a few octaves.

"I don't know. What does it mean to you?"

"A lot. Billy, I have feelings for you. You're my first…" I start to clam up.

"What do you mean that I'm your first?" He asks with eyes wide open.

"I've never felt for anyone what I feel for you. So this means a lot to me." I say watching him look down at his feet.

"Well, you know when I said I've already lost my virginity. Well I lied. You are actually my first too. Even though we haven't done much of anything really…" He says as he continues to look down kicking an imaginary rock on the Church floor board.

For some strange reason, tears started to well up in my eyes and I feel like holding him in the biggest bare hug I could possibly muster. And I do as he takes an unplanned step backwards in utter surprise and bemusement and we both fall down to the floor laughing as a way to release the tension that has been building up...

"Oh, Billy" I start to say while my head rests firmly on his thick chest, "I feel like I want to hold onto you forever." I can hear his accelerated heart rate thumping like wild African drumming in my ears.

"I feel the same way Todd, except my dad...he he wouldn't approve-"

"Shush shush. Forget that right now. Let's just..." I start to say as I look up into his liquid blue eyes and I nearly lost my breath upon seeing just how beautiful he really is, angelic like. I start to get closer to his moist and parted lips until my mouth is fully covering his in a passionate desperate embrace as if this was the last time we are going to see each other. As it turns out and unbeknownst to us, it would be. And he responds with the same intensity. I guess we must have been consumed by the moment because we fail to hear the door opening and a deep thunderous voice bellowing "What is going on here?" We turn around simultaneously to see Father Bogan glaring at us like he just stumbled onto the devil incarnate.

"Dad, I –I-"Billy tries to explain what is so painfully clear to his dad.

"How could you son? How could you let this this b-boy engage you in homosexual behavior," he is fuming at this point. He leaps towards me and grabs my arm and hurls me towards the door all the while hissing "Sinner! Sinner! How could you do this in God's house? Have you no shame? Stay away from my son ya hear! Get out! Get out before I throw you out! You're going straight to hell for this!" He screams at me with wild abandonment. "But dad, it's not his fault. I'm gay dad." Billy says hesitantly. Father Bogan looks at his son with resolute calmness and says "You are dead to me. Go home pack your stuff and leave my house. I intend to tear up your birth certificate. As of this day Sunday March 15th, you no longer exist. "I watch Billy turn as white as a ghost. After listening in horror, I start running as fast as I can towards the exit.

Soon after this incident, Billy moved away. I never heard from him again after that. It's too bad because I think we could have grown up together, loving one another in spite of the hypocritical judgments of his holier than thou dad. Now I understand better why my dads feel the way they do about the Catholic Church. The way I see it, there is enough hate in the world and I cannot imagine that God would punish his sons and daughters for loving one another. And my dads are proof of that love. Their love is so strong, that it is blinding in the face of hatred and prejudice. I eventually come out to my dads, and as expected, they say they love me no matter what. The way I see it, any place where there is love, there is God. Needless to say, I stopped going to St. Mary's. Church for me now is having brunch with my dads on Sunday mornings. Phil Collin's "Take Me Home" plays in my head.

A Candle for Lina

Her skin is like mud, where horses trample
O Can't you see it,
Her skin is like mud, where horses trample
O can't you see it, can't you see it?

In Haiti, misery makes everything pale, grungy, weathered, attenuated, wasteful, sallow, dumb, grinded down, pocketed. When it's done, we swap grinning for crying, we trade tragedy with our brothers so that we can continue to cling to the thinning hairs of the fading forests while gaunt dogs bark defiantly at the scarcity.

When I was a little boy, running around naked in the rain with my cousin Ti Bob, I could always count on Lina to wait for me by the door with a towel in her hands; waiting to dry me off. She was my Restavek; what is known as Nanny here in America. Girls like her gets sent to the city from the country, the land of scarcity; to the city they go, the land of plenty; to live with middle to upper middle class families in Port-au-Prince, Haiti's capital city. Lina was born in 1960, when the then president Francois "Papa Doc" Duvalier still towered over Haiti like an overgrown palm tree; when fear tore souls to pieces and the Haitian vernacular was in handcuffs; when the tongue of oppression lived at the bottom of an empty well; waiting for an echo, waiting for an echo waiting for an echo… to give her voice a chance. She was a short and buxom gal with big African lips and pigeon feet with skin so dark, her teeth almost looked florescent when she grinned and when she walked, it was as if she had a watermelon stuffed on both sides of her hips. She loved to laugh and even laughed sometimes in her sleep; probably while dreaming impossible dreams; only to come awake in the sunny reality of Haiti; amongst the anxious muffles of democracy.

As the sun sets over Port-au-Prince, over Haiti's restive weather, young girls like Lina are sent over from Jacmel and various parts of Haiti's countryside. They tumbled down the Rocky Mountains of Haitian terrains and into the arms of servitude. They are the discarded daughters of misery and scarcity, I watched them cry through their masks at carnivals; I watched them dance the music of political parables made to educate the illiterate; I watched them laugh at their own funerals like zombies in disbelief! Today I remember how we used to play long after they've, turned to clay; forever preserved so that I can remember and so I remember Lina.

Lina worked like a mule, but a grinning mule. I don't even remember her without a smile on her face. She worked from dawn 'til dusk but never without a smile on her face. She woke me up in the morning, helped me get ready for school, made my breakfast and walked me to school, while my mother and father slept in absolute oblivion. Then shortly after noon, she came grinning like the noon day sun to pick me up after school. Once home, she helped me undress, gave me a snack, then cooked my dinner. Then, she fed me dinner, gave me a shower and watched over me as I played with my cousin Ti Bob running and flying kites in our front yard. On occasions when I would fall and scrape my knee, she'd rush to my side, scooped me up in her arms and cradled and rocked me while I cried. Came night time and often during black outs and especially when the moon was out, she would gather up all the kids in the house and regale us with stories of Bouki and Malice, the equivalent to Boris and Morris here in America.

Then one day, long after I left Haiti for America, I heard that Lina went back to the countryside where she came from and died. They said that a voodoo queen killed her over an argument about food in a country where food is scarce. I think she died of a broken heart after I left. But now, she's but a distant memory, but I remember her. I will always remember her completely, her grotesque kind of beauty and her wondrous sense of levity; now she's heavenly and most likely grinning down at me; she will always be a part of me and the following words are in her honor and memory:

I often stop and look at you Lina; you blow my mind; your nappy head don't lie it's where doom takes a nap; Oh, Lina! your breath is bringing down trees you are destroying our planet you are poisoning our wells your children once so much brighter, are still playing with hunger; now you watch them as they grow dimmer ; a box of moonlight shines upon one leaf in need of relief; the moon man has your list; no woman of darkness can resist! oh, Lina; when will you start to wean? your ghosts are disappearing fast; pieces of skies are falling in your lap; the trees are rising and dancing at the funeral you're holding, some people think you're entertaining; thunder's roars are fading substituting our youths for weapons yanked out and fired bang bang bang! your history will rise to watch the offense that offends you take a stand; pandemonium plays in your band; a piece of sky falls cutting the back of your head where your vision center lies; roaring thunder stumbles i could feel it in my gut scorching pieces of weather swim around in your blood; feel free to stab me wear me out and cast me off; you can torch me I'm black so use me like charcoal and burn me; animals will continue to nest in your roots optimism will go on without you; I am a flower so i will continue to blossom; je suis un poet (i am a poet) my roots are embedded deep within the bowels of infinity; when a 3 a.m. plant is damaged at exactly 3 a.m. on the dot it dies of malnutrition simple as that; when some leeches bleed they bathe in their own blood the mockingbird screeches simple as that; but when a mother hen cackles all the cocks fly to be by her side simple as that; in ostracism you start wailing across the Atlantic; you weep an homage to those you left drowning and feeling bereft their breath imports their stories; word of mouth spreads but your ears are burning so you can't hear their cries of fear when Jean Claude "Baby Doc" Duvalier comes near; Every time darkness has a nose drip you get a bowl full of biting dark liquid in your blood stream; mud oozes from your pores; your vision stands stupefied spotting your white coat while you stand protruding from your moat; crows suffocating the epoch pokes at the sun's crux; the day ignites and slants to the right as if on cue before clarity extinguishes it from view; all of our rights are under arrest all of our aspirations can be stuffed in a math box; our voices are weak our tolerance meek but to the weatherman who test northern climates who prepares you for your morning grind in all dimensions who warns you of impending doom-- thunder strikes many times before a storm; when your shrieks break your vocal cords who will be there to operate? when all the surgeons evaporate who will be there to think themselves the man of chance? when thunder finds the rhythm of destruction who will be left to dance? So Lina, start flashing CAUTION! CAUTION! CAUTION!

Her skin is like mud, where horses trample
O Can't you see it,
Her skin is like mud...
...can't you see...?

Cri De Coeur/Cry of the Heart

She was not looking for love when she found him or when he found her. She simply needed a new pair of winter boots that she can wear to be both fashionable and practical. After all, the month of February—already proven to be the whitest winter month—was already teething with more impending snowfall. Enyleve, being from Haiti, have never quite gotten used to Mr. Snowman Winter, even though she had been living in Mattapan for the past twenty-five years. She came to America in her early thirties, now a middle aged woman; she has learned to tolerate a lot of things, particularly Mr. Snowman with his sharp winter teeth ridged with frosty bitterness, always seeming to be ready to bite into her fleshy baby soft brown colored skin.

When she walked into Willy's Wild Shoes in Mattapan Sq., she bore an air of nonchalance. She walked looking straight-ahead, failing to see Willy—who is usually austere by nature—gawking at her from behind his cash register.

"Hello madam. How can I help you today?" He identified her to be Haitian. Maybe because of her plump girth, head wrap, gold jewelry and vibrant colorful attire so typical of most Caribbean women or maybe because there are myriad Haitians who live in the area. When she finally looked to see where the voice was coming from, she became immediately tongue-tied and she had never found herself to be at a lost for words.

"Sssure...I-I was interested in the pair the black leather boots I saw out in the window just now. Do-do you by any chance have it in stock?" She could almost smell the radiant energy emanating from every pore in his short slender white body.

"Mais oui Madame. I do have it in stock. What is your shoe size?" His eyes held her eyes hostage as he spoke all the while not at all trying to conceal the beginning of a swell in the crotch of his pants while he did his best to avoid ogling her sizable breasts. She too began to feel her nipples harden and sensed some moisture in her groin area. After she told him her shoe size, he dashed off to the back to retrieve them. When he returned, she was sitting down with her legs spread apart. Upon seeing her all sprawled out, he dropped the box of shoes. After he regained his composure, he proceeded to take off her shoes so that he could put on the boots. As he was putting on the boots, she bent forward to see how they fit, just as he started to move his head closer and closer to her face. She could feel his hot breath panting like a breathless panther and she responded by reaching down and grabbing his small frame from under his arms and yanked him onto her abdomen and their lips locked together like magnets right there in the store where a customer could have walked in at any given time. Little did they know that that would be the beginning of a torrid five yearlong clandestine affair. Yes, affair. The wedding ring on his left hand confirmed this. He then gave her his card and told her to keep in touch.

When she stepped out into the February night air, she took a deep breath and exhaled some of the sexual tension and excitement she was experiencing. She had never felt such intense instant chemistry with a white man before. She also knew that it was uncommon for women from her cultural background to date outside of their race. Doing so would incur criticism, gossip and in extreme cases ostracism from one's friends, family or community. But none of that mattered to her. She did not mind becoming an iconoclast. She was determined to listen to her heart. But she knew that she would have to keep the relationship hidden like unfashionable clothing in her closet. To her, that only enhanced the sense of excitement and danger.

In Haiti, she had to marry for financial security since the Haitian society dictates that woman is to be subservient to men, who are for the most part the primary breadwinners for their household. Even if a woman is educated, she is still designated as solely a housewife and nothing more. Enyleve's own sister had to forfeit her college degree when the dean, a former friend of her parents, asked her to sleep with him before giving her well earned diploma. For that reason, Enyleve decided to leave everything she'd come to know as her life behind including her domineering and abusive husband and flew like the American eagle towards freedom in America.

On the day of her first date with Willy, she wore her very best outfit, clothes she would normally wear at a wedding, and her fake fur coat to top it all off. She looked into the mirror and for the first time in years, she smiled. Willy made reservations to take her to a local French restaurant called *Rendezvous*. She had by this point in her life, given up on the idea of ever falling in love or even ever meeting someone other than the usual herd of Haitian men, once her former oppressors—that usually vie for her attention to her dismay. She was glad to be living life independently and on her own terms minus the stifling presence of most Haitian men. Both her kids had moved out and she had just turned 40, which to her signified the beginning of the rest of her life.

Willy picked her up dressed in the same clothes in which he spent the entire day getting down on his knees slipping thick leather shoes in the quivering feet of a bunch of libidinous women, who by word of mouth, went to Willy's store because they heard that he often flirts with and become sexually involved with his mostly female clientele. It was a shoe store and sex pit simultaneously. She would found out later just how sexually promiscuous Willy really was. But for now, she was happy to have him: sweaty, somewhat stinky and under dressed.

When they got to the restaurant, Willy kept looking around searchingly and was not acting with the ease and gallantry that she witnessed at his store. Soon after they sat down, Willy began to talk about his wife; about how much he loved her and how he loves their life together with their two kids. She found it peculiar that he was doing this on their first date, but she decided to put teeth marks on her tongue and wait to see where this was going. All through the meal, her heart was doing a sort of elated song and dance. She was brimming with joy, even though she had a sinking feeling that it would not last. After all, how secure can one feel when developing the dreaded "L" word for a married man? But she was as thirsty for love as a dying flower for water. And so she cavaliered along ignoring her womanly intuition, an act that would prove costly down the line.

They never had another date quite like the first one. Willy continued to put forth the fact that he was married the more he saw Enyleve's heart reflected in her eyes whenever she looked at him. Sometimes he would say "We are just two people pleasuring each other, helping one another to meet a sexual need without any strings attached." But Enyleve refused to accept that sex was the only thing happening between her and Willy, even though most of their times together were spent in Enyleve's bedroom. Enyleve not only was Willy's sex toy, but she also offered to be his best friend as well. She encouraged him to tell her **everything** about his excess of sexual escapades with women that dared entered his store. She did this at her own hearts expense. Even though she knew she was falling in love with him, she felt that she would sacrifice her own bleeding heart and listen to his sexual adventures with other women if that helped to keep him in her life. She was also curious about her competition. She wanted to keep him at any cost. One day while Willy was telling her about his marathon of sex with other women, Enyleve began to sharpen two knives she was holding in her hands by grinding them against each other. The more details Willy revealed, the more vigorous the knife sharpening became while her face remained stoical. By that point, Willy started to alternately shift his weight from one leg to the next and his eyes began to do a vertical swing from Enyleve's eyes to her hands until he reached over and grabbed the knives from her hands and slowly led her to the bedroom.

Enyleve knew in her heart that none of the other girls could offer him what she gave him, which was security and freedom in that she had her own place for him to come and go as he pleased and unconditional love, affection, emotional support and friendship. He would often confide in her about matters regarding his family, since his wife and kids were constantly sparing with each other and also would for the most part focus their rage and malcontent towards Willy. Willy also suspected that his wife was having a lesbian affair with her best female friend and also with an Italian policeman who happened to be married to her neighbor. None of this was a problem for Willy because it allowed him the freedom to do as he pleased, and what often pleased him was to stay away from home as much as he could get away with. He would often neglect Enyleve to go out with his latest conquest and would, with unbeknownst insensitivity to her feelings, call to tell her about it the next day. Sometimes she would snap and shout, "That's it! I don't wanna hear any mo 'bout yo cheap bitches! They so easy! All you hav ta do is feed 'em a greasy $1.99 meal just so that you can get yo little white dick sucked in the restaurant parking lot! I bet all those bitches got good DSL too!" Willy looked confused? "That means Dick Sucking Lips!" But sometimes she would simply listen and suffer in silence as the man she loved told her stories of sexual adventures with other women. The disease of knowing often overwhelmed her maligned heart. Sometimes she would flat out tell him not to tell her the details anymore but she would eventually succumb and regress back to her initial burning curiosity. She became addicted to knowing. She became addicted to him. But yet she thought what kind of future she would have with a philandering sex addict. After all, didn't they meet while he was cheating on his wife? After all if he cheated with her, won't he cheat **on** her? He would often manipulate her emotions by constantly complaining about his wife and kids. Particularly his wife whom he often refers to as "The Boss." Nothing he did was sufficient. Nothing he did pleased her. And he would stop at nothing to please The Boss.

One time he told Enyleve about how he celebrated their 25th anniversary by giving her two separate parties. About a year after his ostentations display of his love for her, she refused to sleep in the same bed with him and asked him to sleep in her sewing room on a dilapidated cot. Yet still, he obliged. Yet still he brought her red roses. A gesture he never bestowed upon Enyleve to her chagrin. Their years together grew and at times resembled the similar dysfunction that Willy was experiencing at home mostly because Willy was happy with Enyleve but Enyleve was not happy with Willy.

Over the years Willy and Enyleve broke up numerous times as their relationship became a struggle for power on both parts. Enyleve's struggle for power was mostly to protect herself from Willy's wayward ways. Willy, feeling powerless at home took comfort in having control over his store and the conglomeration of women whom he assumed to be inferior to him in every sense of the word. He always went after Black women from Africa or the Caribbean, of whom he took pleasure in impressing with his store which led them to believe that they've hit the jackpot in landing a seemingly wealthy White man whom they hoped would rescue them from their abject poverty. Willy used the store to ensnare unsuspecting women. Willy was more than glad to let them think what they wished to think. Meanwhile his agenda of using them as a sounding board when he talked of his familial woes and using them as sex objects was always in full bloom. He had managed to mislead all the women who walked into his trap; that is until he met Enyleve who had plans of her own.

When Willy and Enyleve's relationship hit the three year mark, Willy went ballistic! He dived into a waterfall of anger and confusion regarding what was happening between him and Enyleve. He too felt trapped and tricked and told her how he had never went that long with anyone outside of his marriage and that he did not intend to stay in a long term relationship with anyone other than his wife. But Enyleve crept up on him like a mild rash because she wanted to win his heart with her loving, attentive, giving and caring nature in spite of Willy's methodical resistance to feel anything for any of the women with whom he cheated on his wife with. But Enyleve melted his prima facie icy veneer with her unique dose of honeyed legacy, her way of making men feel special by doing things she knows other women would probably not do. She was a good listener, she drew his baths among an array of candle light, she indulged him when he wanted to role play by dressing up in sexy lingerie and she welcomed him into her home to find refuge from the chaos and dysfunction that plagued his

American dream life in the suburbs. Soon he began to see Enyleve as more than just a sex object and more as a romantic partner and even more indispensable friend. However, the relationship had difficulties and limitations that would prove impossible to ignore.

One of their adversities was the fact that Enyleve encouraged Willy to tell her all about his sexual and romantic exploits with other women. Her reason for this was that she did not want to remain in the dark about the man to whom she more or less professed her love. Sometimes she thought about getting a voodoo doll to embody Willy and stick pins in its groin to impede Willy's "sexcapades." Willy relished in the whole scenario. After all this was unheard of. What woman would *want* to know the carnal activities of her man with other women? Willy could not do this with any other women except Enyleve. So Willy was a man who was cheating on his wife, *and* his mistress. Mistress was a title he refused to attribute to Enyleve because of the implications of what that title entailed. Usually a mistress is kept very nicely. Her rent and bills are often taken care of along with the usual accompaniment of gifts. But Enyleve never received any of those things from Willy who also happened to be.... (Drum roll please) **Jewish!** Of course the stereotype of Jews being cheapskates was not far from her mind. Although she did manage to trick him into giving her some things by telling him that some other gentleman callers were offering to buy her gifts. And Willy knew that if he allowed that to happen, then the privilege of being the only male coming in and out of Enyleve's home would be threatened. So he would offer to pay minimally for things whenever he thought the possibility of another lion roaming his den was imminent.

Willy gave her almost anything to keep the position of being the most important man in her life. However, he could not give her what she wanted the most: his heart. He had told her right from the onset of their adulterous union that his heart belonged solely to his beloved wife. Even though he told her how she often disrespected him, disparaged him and berated him in front of his boys. He often felt emasculated by her. But none of those things prevented him from loving her. Even after she had him sleep in a separate room in the house, supposedly for his constant snoring. But like most women, Enyleve thought that if she listened to him enough, pleased him sexually enough, and loved him enough that she could detain his love for his wife for herself. But that never happened in spite of all her efforts.

Eventually the situation of unrequited love between Enyleve and Willy started to take a toll on them both. They started to bicker much like Willy bickered with his wife. In fact, Enyleve became practically like a second wife to Willy. Their once lively and exciting affair eventually started to sour which caused Willy to seek excitement of a new affair with other women, all of lower quality than Enyleve. Willy found Enyleve to be quite fastidious compared to the others whose miniscule expectations were contented if Willy treated them to a cheap greasy meal at some out of the way dingy joint. Unlike Enyleve, they did not demand respect, love, affection and occasional gifts from Willy. Initially, the women thought that they would be treated like Cinderella not knowing that Willy was a typical frugal Jewish and selfish married man who led women on to get his needs met and dump them as soon as they started to make emotional and financial demands on him.

Another issue between Enyleve and Willy was that Enyleve suspected that Willy would avoid taking her out in public because Enyleve was a plus sized middle aged Black woman. All of which Willy denied. He would only take her to little out of the way oasis type places usually in her own neighborhood. If he did take her in a mainstream place where there were a large group of white people, he would act vigilant. "Middle aged men like you don't uzualy go fo women like me. Yo ideal is uzualy petite blond bimbos wit breast up ta dey necks so that you can impress other horny fat middle aged lying and cheatin'assholes like yoself," Enyleve went off on him one day. "You're ashamed to be scene with me! You don't want ta be scene wit a middle aged big Black woman 'cause middle aged class conscious white men like you often go for younger women wit a body you'd mortgage a house for! You're probably going through a mid life crisis and I don't fit the bill! Right? Your friends would not be terribly impressed if they saw you wit me, right?"

she desperately needed assurance. Of course he would deny her accusations.

These arguments often led to temporary break-ups between them. But eventually, they would always get back together. But Enyleve's heart was fragile and could only take so much. She felt that Willy was sucking the blood out of her troubled heart and she was mad at herself for letting him. So like a flower, she slowly began to fold her heart inward and away from Willy's indifference and selfishness until there was nothing left of the relationship but lies, deceit and fits of rage; which sometimes set the stage for some bed shaking, mouth drooling, eyes watering and sweat dripping make-up sex between them. The love she once felt had been watered down to practically nothing. They never remained friends like Willy suggested. It turned out that Willy did not want friendship minus the possibility of sex. "Typical man" Enyleve thought. After their final break-up, Enyleve still consumed by thoughts of vengeance and malice decided to make a midnight run to his store and spray painted "FREE SEX WITH EVERY PURCHASE!!!" on his storefront window.

Enyleve wanted to renew her spirits after the dramatic break-up with Willy so she decided to give herself an internal diagnosis to see what it is about her that was attracting these types of defunct men in her life. Maybe it's her motherly aura. All her life she has always cared for others. She cared for her sisters after her parents died, her alcoholic ex-husband, her kids and then her grandchildren. She never made time for herself. So then she revolted against all who had unwittingly and willfully imprisoned her, including herself. She also got a physical make-over by changing her hairdo, joined a gym and bought new exciting clothes to celebrate her newfound freedom. She joined a social network on the net called Meetup.com so that she can share things in common with a group of people in her neighborhood. Life then to her seemed new and refreshed and the possibilities endless. She decided to date herself for a change, she made herself the love of her life instead of waiting for a man to make her life complete. And then one day, while attending one of her social groups, a man, who seemed very well put together, approached her. She smiled with unmitigated confidence and said "My name is Enyleve. It's a pleasure for you to meet me…" as she tilted her head back in joy and laughter.

These days she has adjusted to what she used to fear: the caustic bite of Mr. Snowman Winter. On stormy days, she puts on the leather boots that brought her and Willy together and bravely trudges through the February snow. On a clear day, if you look close enough, you can see the sun rising in her eyes.

The Reason Why Crickets Chirp

Inspired by my niece Natavia Bouquet who explained it to me

It's just about midnight and I'm feeling too good to sleep. I sit up on the bed, hug my knees to my chest and stare at my husband Jean-Joseph sleeping next to me. He's only been in this country for the last five years. Before that he was in Haiti; that is until I did everything in my power to bring him to America. While living in Haiti, we met in high school and became fast friends. We soon became inseparable. He was my high school sweetheart. He was my first love and I'm fervently hoping that he will be my last. We both come from middle class families, which explain why we met at an exclusive private school in Port-au-Prince, Haiti, where both our families lived. There are five offspring in my family, all girls and I'm the first born. I suppose I should feel lucky to have been born in Haiti's capitol city because my mother told me that in the countryside, girls are not sent to school; only boys get to attend school. If you think that's absurd, the reason is even more so. You see, parents came up with the theory that if they keep the girls from becoming learned, then they will not be able to communicate with boys by means of love letters etc....That way, the parents get to keep their female offspring under control with the ultimate goal being to ensure that the girls keep their virginity until they marry. Meanwhile, the parents make sure that the female offspring are learning the domestic duties that essentially keep a house hold running; thus preparing them for their future husbands. So I am very grateful to have been born in the city to civilized and educated parents.

After staring at Jean-Joseph for quite some time, I get out of bed, fumble in the dark for my bedroom slippers and tip toe out of the bedroom leaving the door ajar so not to wake up Jean-Joseph. I make my way down the dimly lit hallway to my daughter Viatana's bedroom. The door squeaks as I open it. Once inside, I walk over slowly to hover over my sleeping beauty of a daughter, tucked in neatly under her purple fairytale sheet and blanket. I smile with a sense of exaggerated joy, thankful for my new life in America. However, things weren't always easy. So find yourself a comfortable seat, kick back and let me tell you my story.

I arrived in the United States in 1994 with nothing but a tepid smile and a suitcase full of hope of a new beginning. Contrary to popular belief, I did not come on a boat but on American Airlines. New York was my first pit stop and I eagerly smiled when I saw the towering and hopeful presence of the Statue of Liberty. I came from a country that debase, disparage and subjugate women. So it was a welcomed change to bask at the dignified grandeur and emblem of freedom and opportunity that reflect the Statue of Liberty. I had no definite destination when I arrived at the airport. I did know that I had a second cousin who lived in Brooklyn. So I decided to pay her a surprise visit, hoping that she'd take me in, even if it's out of pity and guilt since she was family. When I got there, no one was home. So I just waited in the park across the street. I went back to the door just a little after 6pm.

"Who is it?" A woman's voice bellowed reluctantly.

"Marnine, it's me Yolande! Your cousin. I just arrived from Haiti. I can't wait to see you! Can I come in?" I tried to sound gladder to hear her voice than I actually was. We were never that close and there was plenty of family rivalry drama between us that further soured our kinship.

"Oh. Yolande! Come up pitite come up!" She blended Creole with English as most Haitian Americans do when they talk. She greeted me with a huge bear hug and said, "Come in, pitite, Come in." I told her my story and she agreed to let me stay until I get on my feet by finding a job and eventually my own place to live. But things didn't go as planned. Her lothario husband became particularly fond of me and Marnine accused me of purposefully seducing him. Hey, it wasn't my fault that I was young, beautiful with breasts up to my neck. I was used to enduring the wrath of intimidated women, but I also understood that that came with the curse of being a fatal beauty.

Unbeknownst to Marnine, Jean-Bernard, her husband, rented me a room in a friend's apartment, gave me some pocket money and promised to help me find a job. All I had to do was accompany him to parties and concerts so that his friends could see him with a beautiful younger woman on his arms. I was basically a trophy with a price tag and that was fine with me, since I had no other means of survival. Meanwhile, the husband of the woman I was staying with also fell in love with my youthful beauty. So this was going to be yet another ménage a trois of which I did not anticipate being part of. One day I came home earlier than usual from pounding the pavement looking for work to find the woman's husband rolling around naked and obviously aroused over my entire lingerie collection on my bed. Suffice it to say, I told Jean-Bernard about the situation and he soon rented me a place in a rooming house, where I encountered a whole set of other woes and calamities.

Jean-Bernard found me found me a job at a candy factory. I was so elated that I leaped onto him and showered him with grateful kisses which he responded to by growing a stiff machete in his trousers. That night, we celebrated our growing contentment in my small and cozy room. The next day, I had trouble looking myself in the mirror. I took a shower and scrubbed my skin raw all the while thinking about my true love back in Haiti. I found consolation in telling myself that I was doing this for "us" and that he never needs to know about my own private sacrifices. Besides, how was I to know whether he was finding comfort in the arms of one of those lascivious Haitian hussies. I also found consolation in reading my bible and praying before bed every night.

Things were good at work for quite some time; that is until my obnoxious White boss decided to taunt me daily because, as I would later find out, he was crazy in lust with me. One day he came by my working station, gave me a leering look, lowered his snarly lips to my ear and said, "Is it true that you Caribbean women often have gigantic pussies and an even bigger bush?" He then straighten up, took a step back so that I could get a look at his pinky finger sized erection, slapped my derriere and walked away. That night, I cried myself to sleep due to overwhelming feelings of anger and humiliation. I decided to tell Jean-Bernard about the whole ordeal and he strongly advised me to file a sexual harassment lawsuit against my boss. I eventually filed a lawsuit with a lawyer that agreed to only charge me a fee if he wins. We ended up winning particularly because there were plenty of other women who were willing to come forward with similar stories of harassment against my boss. We ended up walking away with a hundred thousand dollars from my boss's company. My lawyer took 20 percent and I end up using the rest of the money to put down on a house and send for Jean-Joseph in Haiti.

We ended up buying a home in upstate New York. Jean-Joseph got his teaching degree while working as a Teacher's Aid since he was already a teacher in Haiti and we soon had Viatana. I told Jean-Bernard that I had to cut all ties with him since he was now part of my past; a past that I'm not too proud of and that Jean-Joseph is now part of my present and future. He reluctantly agreed and said he will miss me. So now I suppose I am living the American Dream, which came at a great cost to me and my family. They don't tell you that in the "Come to America" propaganda do they?

One night my daughter Viatana and I were sitting on the front porch and the moon shone bright through the darkness of our quiet suburban life. The only sounds we heard were that of our breath and the chirping of crickets. Then suddenly Viatana uttered "Mommy do you know why crickets chirp?" I was simultaneously amused and intrigued by her question. "Uhhh...because they're hungry?" I said with raised eyebrows. Then without hesitation she said, "No. Because they are happy." I was thoroughly flabbergasted this coming from a four year old. I reached over and pulled her closer to me as tears well up in my eyes. "Mommy, why are you crying?" She asked with child like concern. "Because I'm happy baby. I'm crying because I'm happy."

The Whistler's Song

It was a dark and gloomy Sunday. Charlotte Cherveau Von Zabern was just wiggling herself awake next to her husband Tom, a white man from Germany whom she'd met on the train to work one day. Charlotte herself is from Haiti. Her parents brought her and her brother to America when she was just 5 years old and her Whizzy was 14. Her childhood felt pure and dreamlike, that is until tragedy the tragedy.

They settled in rural Whitey, Mississippi back in 1955, during the cusp of the civil rights movement and racial tensions were as high as the tallest trees in the forests. Charlotte never even knew that she was herself a "nigger" until it was pointed out to her by the local white kids and even some of the adults, who made it very clear that they did not want her kind playing with their blond haired blue eyed children. One day, she ran home to her mother crying that the neighboring kids were calling her a "nagger." Her mom under-reacted and simply told her "You are a beautiful dark skinned princess. God loves you and created you in his image and don't you ever forget it. Just tell those kids that God loves all of us just the way he made all of us and simply walk away."

Whizzy on the other hand was getting in all sorts of fights with some of the white boys who called him a nigger. He just could not control his temper despite the accompanying danger that came with expressing it. Yolande, their mother, gave him the same speech she had slowly deposited in Charlotte's head. But Whizzy was impervious to her words. And so one day, while Whizzy was walking home from school with a group of his friends, a white woman was walking in the opposite direction. Whizzy whistled at her, failing to recognize that in those days it was considered unacceptable for a Black man to even glance at a white woman with eyes of desire, let alone whistle at her. Word must have strewn about what Whizzy had done because vengeance caught up to him one night while he was walking home alone one evening coming from the spring dance at school. It was a full moon and all Whizzy could hear were the sounds of his feet on the rocky path and the chirping of crickets keeping him company on his journey. And as usual, he was whistling a tune that the night could fall at sleep to. Walking was one of his favorite physical activities. He enjoyed the serenity, a soothing remedy to his usually restless spirit. Then suddenly, he heard hurried feet behind him, trying to catch up to him and by the time he turned his head to see who it was, the last thing he saw was a baseball bat meeting his forehead and the last words he heard before he blacked out was "filthy nigger! Yah gonna pay."

After Whizzy's death, Yolande and her husband Andre decided to leave the south and move to the north, where she was told was more progressive in their thinking, particularly in matters of race and ethnicity. They decided to move to Boston, Massachusetts, in a Boston neighborhood named Mattapan. There, they would encounter a more subtle kind of racism and gang violence but still managed to stay safe.

Charlotte left her husband in bed to prepare their usual Sunday morning brunch. Tom made it very clear to Charlotte that he expects a strict adherence to order and structure and treated her like his own private possession. Tom insisted on putting iron bars in the first floor windows of the house even though they lived in the suburbs. Charlotte would often find herself staring through the bars and out in the open fields where she daydreamed of running against the wind with the wind in her hair and the sun on her face. As tears started to well up in her eyes, she tried to convince herself that she was happy with Tom. After all, didn't she have what most people coveted: The suburban house with the picket fence, two cars in the driveway and two dogs running blissfully in her vast yard? But Tom's moods were often erratic. One minute he would be affectionate and turned verbally abusive the next; often calling Charlotte a "fat blob who didn't know her head from her ass" whenever she failed to obey one of his orders. Charlotte would rarely reflect about why she married a man like Tom because she did not want to face the fatal truth behind her decision. A truth that went back to the day she lost her brother Whizzy to hatred, malevolence and intolerance. She felt proud to be seen in public with Tom. She often found herself looking around to see who was staring at her. She even distanced herself from the company of other Black people. She clanged desperately to Tom's friends and relatives so that she could continue to walk around with her head held high in the blue eyed sky. One day, Tom asked "How come you don't have any Black friends?" She turned her head away, looked down at her shuffling foot and said "I have Black friends... you've just never met them."

She never told Tom about how her beloved whistler brother Whizzy died. She did not even want to think about it anymore. Like the tragedy happened to someone else, to an unfortunate Black family that she is no longer part of. She was enjoying living the American Dream in the suburb of Lakeville, Massachusetts. Her parents still live in what is now notoriously known as Murderpan instead of Mattapan due to the increasing crime rate. In the spring of 1984, she became pregnant with her first child. They soon learned that they were having a boy, to both their delights. Charlotte wanted to name him Whizzy but Tom wanted to name him William. So they compromised. The child would be named William "Whizzy" Von Zabern.

William Whizzy was very much akin to Charlotte's brother Whizzy. He was an unapologetic recalcitrant as well as being an adventurer with a carefree "joie de vivre"attitude. He loved playing with the neighborhood kids. The fact that he was the only Black kid in the neighborhood did not seem to matter to the other kids. They were swept up in the whirlwind of his jovial attitude and charisma.

One day, William Whizzy wondered off into the woods and unbeknownst to him, onto someone else's property. It was a lazy Sunday afternoon and so he decided to rest under a weeping willow tree. The next thing he knew, he was jolted awake by a white man with some type of rifle pointed to his face. "What the hell yah doin' on mah propty nigger?" He spat out as his eyes turns into a pool of blood like he was the devil incarnate. William Whizzy opened his mouth to try to explain himself but was interrupted. "Don't even say nothin' nigger. I leegally have a right to shoot yah. Just get yah nigger ass off mah propty!" As William Whizzy got up to leave, his legs felt feeble and weak like a baby just learning to walk. He ran home without looking back.

In an avalanche of hurried speech, he related to Charlotte what happened. Charlotte covered her mouth and her head sank into her chest as she broke into a river of tears. All the ghostly memories of her past came pouring out of her to the point of being un-consolable. When she told Tom what happened he simply said "Serves him right for being at the wrong place at the wrong time." Charlotte was flabbergasted by his reaction. How could he not even care that his own flesh and blood was affronted, berated and disparaged by the "N" word with a gun to his face no less? Suddenly, a storm cloud imploded inside of her. She didn't say or do anything right then. Later on that week, Tom came home to a near empty house except for his own possessions that was left behind. Charlotte had pulled and emergency exit release lever and catapulted herself and William back home to the succoring and welcoming arms of her parents. She wanted to live life on her own terms. First thing she wanted to do was make peace with her troubled past; which included coming to terms with being a Black woman in white America. On one particular day, she passed by a mirror and smiled. Something she hadn't done in a very long time.

Once on a sunny day, she went out to an open field carpeted by the greenest green you've ever seen, running with the sun on her face, the wind in her hair and whistling a familiar tune in her ears.

What I Should Have Said

I just could not bear it any longer. The anticipation. It has been twenty years since I last saw her. Since the incident. *Then* she was just a whirlwind of beauty; a paragon of temptation. She had silky blond locks that barely grazed the top edge of her supple shoulders and it caught the sunlight just right. Her smile was like morning: fresh, inviting and hopeful. She was earth mother. She was moon. She was sky.

I met her during the mid sixties, in the midst of the flower power movement in the backdrop of the Vietnam War in a commune in San Francisco. The first day I saw her she was crouched in front of a neighboring river. I came up behind her, as softly as the flow of the water, taking pleasure looking down at her. She was so close to the river that I could see her wobbly reflection in the shifting water. I just stood there enjoying her harmony; wishing that I could freeze the moment forever. Just me and her in this Eden by the river. She must have noticed me through her peripheral vision because without even looking back she said, "Well, yah just gonna stand there or yah gonna make your move?" I was startled by her boldness. I became immediately enchanted. "Ahhhh…I'm…I'm… sorry. I didn't mean to disturb you…"

"Puh…leasse, save it." She turned to look at me. "So let me see. You strike me as a charmer. A total ladies man and you think yourself better looking than you really are and you use your looks and gallantry to get what you want. Am I right or am I right?" She asked smilingly.

"I…I…" I swallowed down her words.

"I…thought so," she said with a self-congratulatory bobbing of her head.

"So go head, ask me out. Maybe I'll say yes," she said enticingly. Never before have I *not* been in control in a situation involving a female. She threw me a curve ball, like seeing the moon in the middle of the day.

"So, will you? Go out with me?" I said with a tepid smile.

"Sure. Why not? I could use a good laugh." With that she stood up, shook her flowery skirt, extended her delicate hands to me and said, "Lead the way Valentino." I didn't know where we were going, but for the first time in my life, I didn't care.

We decided to cohabitate. I tried to ignore how she often looked at me; like she was afraid that I would hurt her. Neither one of us ever mentioned the "L" word. We would often get into feverish altercations that would eventually erupt with her up against the wall, panting as I kissed her lips, neck and groped her coconut-sized breasts with insatiable intensity. The fights soon became the best parts of our tumultuous relationship because they would almost always lead to sex. She thought that I was always looking at other women. Well, ok, she was right. But every man deserves the benefit of the doubt at some point during his philandering life, right? Anyways, no man was ever met to be with just one woman. It's in our biological make-up. Look it up.

Then one morning, she fed me a pregnancy pronouncement for breakfast. She wanted to abort it. I wanted her to keep it. But she insisted, saying it was *her* decision to make and I ruefully supplied the money. It was the worst day of my life. I left and never looked back. Then one day, she found me on Facebook and here I am, waiting at an intersection, somewhere in San Francisco. Then she came. Still slender. Still blond. Still beautiful. But she looked sorrowful.

"Hi Rocky," she said looking down at her feet, minus her former grace and illustriousness.

"Hi," I said embarrassed by her diminutive presence.

"Well, don't yah wanna know what it's been like fo' me fo' the last twenty years after you left?"

"I...I...." I felt as awkward as a teenager on a first date.

"I cried every night for five months!" She screamed. "Did you know that my dad left us on my sixtieth birthday? Did you know that you were my first?" My mouth hung open. "Yeah, well you were! I got diagnosed with cervical cancer so I can't ever have another baby! You were older than me! You should have talked me out of it you sonofabith! I loved you you idiot! You shouldn't have left! You shouldn't have…" She covered her face and started weeping like an inconsolable child. And I didn't know what to say. She then made a swift turn and started running away from me.

I just stood there, flabbergasted. But what I wanted to say was, "I'm sorry. I'm sorry for stealing your virginity. Sorry for disrespecting you by looking at other women in your presence. Sorry I never said I loved you. Sorry for not talking you out of aborting our baby. Sorry for not telling you that you are the most of all the rest, the *most*. Sorry for not marrying you. Sorry for using you for my own selfish sexual gratification. Sorry for leaving you. Please forgive me. Please…" But I just stood there, at an intersection somewhere in San Francisco, remembering what I could no longer see; as her wobbly reflection in the water danced in my memory; now forever and ever **frozen**.

The Naughty Mamas' Book Club

Jislene scurries around her apartment determined not to be defeated by the Haitian Time Curse to always be late. She is married to a White man and living—what looks like to most outsiders—the American dream in the suburb of Lakeville, Massachusetts while her only daughter is away at University.

Now, in her red convertible with the top down and the wind in her straight black hair, she is listening to Tracy Chapman's "Fast Car" from her debut album just released. She sings along with the lyrics: "You got a fast car; maybe together we can get somewhere. Maybe we make a deal, starting from nothing got nothing to lose…" She smiles to herself as she anticipates seeing the girls since they only meet once a month.

First there is Gilda, a gregarious gal who's constantly laughing, even at things most people don't even find funny. Betsy is a yoyo dieter. Her husband often mocks her by making "BooBoom Booboom Booboom" sounds when she walks in public, which Betsy always pretends to laugh off and then cries herself to sleep at night. Wanda, an Arabic woman who always wears a head wrap and covered up in layers of clothes leaving only her face and hands visible to the public, to appease her Arabic husband. Polish Paula, at 25 with blond hair and blue eyes, is the youngest of the group with a curvaceous hour glass figure that most middle aged men would mortgage a house for.

Jislene arrives just as the sun is setting over her rural surroundings. She pushes through the door left ajar with an apologetic half smile on her face for always being late. "Bonsoir and sorry ladies, I really tried hard not to be late this time," she says in her Haitian accent.

"Oh, Jislene. Next time, I'll have to send a time police to your house to handcuff you and bring you here on time?" Gilda utters laughingly.

"Sweety, you think I would waste my time with you bitches if you sent me a uniformed stallion to play with?" Jislene tilts her head back and laughs.

"Ladies, I take it you all have finished the book? I know I did and it was a fascinating read please, sit," Betsy declares. "I particularly like the title 'Mother, Lover, Murderer.' I also found it to be quite relevant to the plight of modern women to free themselves from male domination, don't you?" They all sit in Betsy's living room and commence sipping tea and coffee.

"Oh, yes...I've known plenty of women who have been pushed to the edge to...you know, have reason to kill," says Jislene as she looks nervously around the room, avoiding direct eye contact with the other women while she sips her coffee.

"I found the sex scenes to be quite tantalizing indeed...." Wanda chuckles as she looks around at the women.

"You of all people? Walking around all covered up like a mummy? You almost had me thinking that all you do in bed is pray!'" says Jislene, which invokes laughter from the women.

"My favorite part was when Marla murdered her husband. I think it was justified since he practical enslaved her. I mean, who ties someone's arms and legs to bed posts and then continuously act out mock rape scenes just for kicks and then afterwards expect her to cook his dinner and draw his bath. I would kill the motherfucker too if I was in that situation." Spitballs are flying out of Jislene's mouth and the veins in her neck are visibly throbbing as she practically barks out the words. Wanda squirms uncomfortably in her seat as she watches Jislene speak. Gilda laughs, but it almost seems forced. And at that very moment, a hissing sound can be heard coming from the kitchen, and Betsy—welcoming the distraction—stands up and asks, "More tea anyone?" Everyone said no.

"Well, I definitely think that the son of a bitch got what he deserved," offers Paula. "Now you can understand why I use my looks to manipulate the hell out of those assholes and clean out their bank accounts by the time I am done with them. Sex appeal is my ultimate weapon against those pigs and he better be packing no less than eight and a half inches if he wants to slip his key into *my* lock." Paula tilts her head in a brief forward and backward motion to accentuate her point. And all the women drop their jaws and raise their eyebrows in Paula's direction.

"Well, my Charlie has his asshole moments, especially when he pokes fun of my weight, but for the most part he is good to me. As long as I do what he wants and try not to piss him off with back talk, we're good. So what if he wants me to cook and clean in full make-up and high heels when he is around. I like to surrender to his 1950's housewife fantasies," Betsy says in a low resigned voice. As the ladies take turns talking, the moon can be seen hovering behind a cloud outside the living room window and the sizzling summer night air, which has seeped into the house—feels stifling and Betsy responds by turning on the ceiling fan.

"My husband is fucking my brother!" Wanda exclaims and all eyes turn to her in shock and disbelief. "As you know my brother has been staying with me since his divorce. Now I know why the marriage didn't work!" The ladies are all silent and shocked. Paula speaks first, "Your macho male chauvinist husband? What makes you think…I mean…do you have any proof?"

"Well, one day I came home and my brother came out of our bedroom bare-chested, sweaty and buttoning up his pants, and I could hear Slav scurrying around our bedroom and when I quickly poke my head in, he too was half naked trying to get his pants on. They both said half in unison that they were just wrestling with each other. Which I thought was a crack of shit!" Wanda leans forward with her right hand on her right thigh and cupped under her chin as she looks down at the floor. Outside, the moon is still slowly trying to evade the dense cloud that obliterates it and the windows are illuminated slightly by its florescent glow and rattling a bit from the growing wind. All the women are silent for a brief moment and the sound of crickets can be heard coming from the nearby woods. "What are you gonna do now Wanda?" Gilda asks.

"I don't know. The women in my family never even consider divorce" Wanda says as she looks off in the distance. And then suddenly, like she just became infused with a sudden boost of manic energy, declares "But you know what, I think I'm gonna be the first. I'm going to divorce his faggot ass!" Then she stands up, yanks the head wrap from her head, takes off the long robe to expose a tight strapless red dress she wore underneath and all the women gasps in utter bewilderment and then suddenly begin clapping while Wanda takes a number of bows as if she'd just given the performance of a lifetime. "This is the kind of clothes I am going to wear from now on," she says in a triumphant fashion. And with that, they adjourned the meeting.

As Jislene drives home, she is content to think that the ladies don't really know that she had been raped and sexually abused by her dad—while her mother looked the other way—since she was just five years old to the age of sixteen when she finally mustered the courage to run away from home. They don't know that she has been physically and mentally abused by every man she'd ever married since running away from home, including her current one. They think they know who wrote the book they just read. She bears a knowing smirk as she shift the gears of her standard, the moon finally peaks from the under the heavy handed mass of clouds to illuminate the dark highway on which she had driven many times on her way home from her book club.

The Dark Night of the Soul

Benny stares through his basement window and he can feel his heart rejoicing once again by the absence of the sun. The sun has become his worst enemy since his parents died, his wife left him and his only son has been officially declared MIA (missing in action) while fighting the war in Iraq. These days, he hardly leaves his apartment. He closes all the shades, draws all the curtains and turns off all the lights while he just lies on his back with his hands clasp behind his head and his eyes transfixed at the white ceiling. Sometimes he lays with his back to all the stuff he has accumulated over the years. Stuff that he can't seem to bring himself to get rid of. He likes to rummage through other people's trash and bring various things to his already cramped space. There is so much stuff in his place that there's hardly any room for *himself*. Clothes carpet his floors, empty take-out boxes are all piled up in one corner of his bedroom next to the TV and there are a number of shopping bags filled with trash rotting in the kitchen and maggots have taken residence under them. His window overlooks the sky and he often feels like God is looking down on him. The phone lately has been ringing with a sort of desperate urgency, yet Benny remains completely still as if he hasn't heard it at all and just lets the machine deal with the incessant calls. His friends, or at least the few he has managed to hold on to, must be wondering about where he is. He has once before tried to end it all by starving himself of food and water for nearly two weeks. But at the last minute changed his mind and decided to have a can of coke and a slice of pizza.

He has ceased to maintain any sort of personal care and he is beginning to smell. His apartment has a stale order of decay swirling lazily around the air. The smell is akin to rat and mice droppings, if you've ever had the misfortune to smell that particular odor. There are litters of unwashed dishes in the sink, mold all over his bathroom walls, a mail box full of unopened mail and a mass of newspapers piled up in front of his door. From an outsider's point of view, it would seem as if no one lives there at all. Day after day, Benny just lies there, living a death in life with nothing to look forward to or get up out of bed for. "What a waste," he thinks to himself. "Just taking up space." Death seems to be constantly tip toeing around him, waiting for the right time to finish him off.

He remembers happier times when his wife Lola sat in the sand on the beach on Martha's Vineyard building a sandcastle with their son, little Jimmy. Her long straight Brown hair flirting and twirling in the summer wind while Little Jimmy screeches with joy and laughter "Daddy look! Look Daddy. I made a castle! I made a castle!" He remembers looking on and smiling with an open book on his lap and thinking how complete his life is finally, as the summer wind gently lifts his blond hair off his forehead. He remembers feeling the joy of a man who constantly keeps winning the lottery over and over again every time he thinks about his life with his beloved family. His parents were still alive back then and they used to go visit then on the cape where they all lived. But his bouts with depression and psychosis have driven his wife away. She could no longer tolerate his bouts of rage and paranoia that plagues him when his ill. She begged and pleaded with him to seek treatment, but he refused to admit that he is even sick at all. Eventually, his denial and the ensuing consequences drove her away. She feared that had she not left him, she would start hating him and she could not contend with that possibility. So inspite of herself, she left and took little Jimmy with her. That actually exacerbated his already declining mental health. She had custody and he had the weekends. His visitations became less and less regular as his life careened out of control due to his untreated mental condition. Before he knew it, Little Jimmy turned eighteen and joined the army. He had an on again and off again relationship with Lola. On when he was well, off when he was not.

Now lonely and bereft of emotion, he lies motionless on his disheveled bed staring at the ceiling of his sinister apartment waiting for something, anything to happen to make him feel alive again. He used to be a man who *made* things happen; now he has become a man who *waits* for things to happen. He used to walk around with a half smile on his face, a twinkle of joy and mischief in his eyes and a restless eagerness in his steps. He used to be the life of the anywhere he happens to be, always ready to crack a joke or laugh at someone else's. He used to pretend to walk around like a sad man with his head hanging over his chest, and then all of a sudden perk right back up again laughing at himself. Now, he feels that his fire has been snuffed out by a giant bright red hand that has descended directly from hell.

The phone is ringing again and it goes directly to the machine. "Hey Benny! It's George. What's goin' man? I haven't heard from you in days. I'm starting to worry. Call me." He lies still unresponsive. He decides that tomorrow he will do something, anything, even though he does not know what it is. He'll find out when he actually does it.

The next day, a streak of sunlight slices his bedroom floor and for the first time in months, he does not mind its shiny glare. "Today's forecast is expected to be sunny and temperatures are expected to reach record high for March." His listens to his clock radio as he gets out of bed. For the first time in months he has decided to clean himself up. He showers, shaves, puts on clean clothes and even cleans his dirty apartment. He opens his night stand and grabs his rosary beads. He makes the sign of the cross using his middle finger first on his forehead, then chest then his left and right shoulders. He then says a quiet prayer then leaves the apartment. He passes in front of the mirror and smiles at himself as he heads out. He gets on the train and heads and finds himself getting off at the stop near the beach, the same beach he used to spend time with his family. He spends all day at the beach, watching happy families, seagulls and listening to the soothing sounds of the waves. He is waiting for darkness to fall and soon, the sun descends into the belly of the sea and everyone has left the beach. He lies in the sand on his back with his hands clasped behind his head as he stares into the dark skies, which he feels promises him nothing. At midnight, he gets up and walks toward the sea. The voices of his wife and son echoes in his ears from that perfect summer day he remembers so well—"Daddy look! Look Daddy!"—as he enters the sea until he is completely submerged to dwell forever in its abyss. Just then, back home his wife left him a message about possibly getting back together if he's willing to go into treatment, his son is leaving him a message announcing his homecoming and the moon emerges to hover over the sea and diminish the darkness. His soul wishes he was there to come and see.

Sultry Boy

"No testing has overtaken you that is not common
to everyone. God...will not let you be tested
beyond your strength, but with the testing he
will also provide a way out so that you may be
able to endure it."

1 CORINTHIANS 10.13

You never notice that our parents almost always come home just when we're bored enough to be doing something wrong? Is that God's way of making sure that we adhere to the teachings of the Ten Commandments? "Honor thy mother and thy father..." Now whose **not** guilty of falling short of this most earnest bit of wisdom? What about sex? What do the commandments say about sex? As far as I know it's no sex before marriage, is that right? As wound up, bible clutching, cross bearing grandmothers would say, "Sex is for procreation not recreation..." Along with that comes the Catholic guilt! Yes, I got my start as an uptight catholic fart. And we all know that a fart doesn't need any religion for it to stink, right? I was in catholic school up until the seventh grade. I walked catholic, talked catholic, feared sex like Catholics, and yes even farted catholic.

You know what I'm talking about, the "silent shameful" deadly fart, the kind like SIN unleashed like hissing serpents in a hot crowded church, while big fat black Creole woman sing songs of hope and praise, while wiping their putrid sweat pouring down their fat sweltering faces, as the minister's shouts of condemnation showers and wilds the audience with his funky breath mouth swollen with his sanctimonious sermon in a fever pitch voice begging the crowd for an AMEN! With that as my backdrop, let me regale you with a story of a cascading catholic city boy gone wild!!!

To the chagrin of my family and yes sadly even sometimes to myself, **I am gay**. There I said it! I am watching the cursor on my computer still blanking, waiting for me to elaborate. The world didn't end. I -am- gay. So what? Right? It's not like admitting that I am gay makes **you** gay, right? Unless you in the closet? Well, **are** you? Anyways, my father thought that I was a little "soft" so to speak, so he enrolled me in an all male school full of Jesuit priests to make a **man** out of me, where boys with burgeoning manhoods were erect with insatiable sexual curiosities. In case you didn't know, Jesuits are a member of the Society of Jesus, a Roman Catholic religious order affianced in worldly missionary and pedagogical activity. The order was spearheaded by Saint Ignatius Loyola in 1534 during the Renaissance—which is a period in history which included cultural and religious revival—with the purpose of protecting Catholicism against Reformation. One of the things we used to do first thing Monday mornings was to yank each other's pants down to see whose pistols grew bigger and whose didn't. And we'd humiliate the ones who **didn't**. It's a wonder I'm not a "size queen" today because of it!

The other thing we used to do in catholic school was to compare stories about who **haven't** played with their nannies yet? Most of us were from middle class families to be at that school, so we knew that almost all of us had nannies. In Haiti that's called rites of passage, in America it's called child abuse. I remember experimenting with sex with my nanny during one of our usual black outs. My cousin Tod and I did her together. We went into her darkened room just as she was lighting up her candles.

"Hi boys, what ya upta?" we could see Nali's white teeth against the darkness.

"Nothing." we tried to be coy.

"Well come on you two, come give Nali a little massage. I know yall came here for something."

Tod took the top I took the bottom. Nali was on her back, her favorite position, my grandma Mini once said. Tod fooled around with her balloons and I fooled around with her cat. We had cute names for girlie parts then. I remembered it stinking so good that I didn't wash my middle finger for a solid week. I think that's when I discovered that I was a sniffer.

I love funky sweaty starving smells. Although, as I grew older, I developed more of a taste for the smell of a man more so than for the smell of a woman. As a kid, I used to get very close to the male porters delivering cargoes to our house in Haiti so to inhale them. They wouldn't have on any shirts, underwear, deodorant or shoes. Just a pair of tight fitting jeans hugging coconut sized buttocks rippling, their masculinity straining through the fabric, long streaks of cooling sweat oozing down tickling their crotches toying with my fancy, slick sizzling licks of heat racing down their hung tree trunk thighs. Most rich gay men here in the states wouldn't think twice to mortgage a house for a trunk of hunk like this!

I also suspected my homosexuality when I found myself wrestling. A lot! The idea of two males grunting and rubbing and pegging each other down to the floor yelling "you give?" just appealed to me. So I wrestled. As many people as I could. My favorite was the son of my aunt's husband, Tobert! He was sent to the city directly from the country, with the hay still inside his dusty sandals, he too with heavy swinging country grown Haitian thighs. He had a habit of walking around with only his shirt on and nothing else, en route to taking a bath. That's when Tod and me would catch him, locked the doors and wrestled him down. Our collective "boyhoods" would become erect with youth juice and eventually; one of us would have to squirt. Usually it was Tobert. Boy how sweet that boy came! Tod and I would wince at the sight of him relieving himself! It was like watching him milk a cow or something!! This wrestling business became a habit. Soon enough we started skipping church to hang out at the movie theatre all day long waiting for Jackie Chan movies. Back then we liked Jackie

Chan but simply feared the Catholic Church! So we opted for the former. Jackie Chan ruled our Sundays!

I left Haiti when I was 10 years old. I made the mistake of thinking that I'd left all that the Catholic Church represented behind when I came to the U.S. I was wrong. So **so** wrong. Sex to me became synonymous with guilt, shame, fear, and a sense of *disgust.* I found myself thrown into a school environment with both sexes and I even felt more pressured in the mixed American school then when I was in the all boy catholic school in Port-au-Prince, Haiti. The boys for "hanging too much with the girls" teased me and the girls teased me for not being like "one of the boys." So I was caught between a rock and a hard place. I felt such an intense attraction towards the boys that I could not risk being around them for fear of being found out! There was this particular white boy from the baseball team. I would see him coming from practice, dripping sweltering like sex on legs! And somehow my crotch would rise to salute him as he struts by stroking and twirling this giant baseball bat in his King Kong hands!

One of the ways I vented my frustrations was to play "blind man" during swim class. I never wore goggles so I swam with my eyes closed. So I would end up "feeling" as many "boys" under the water as humanly possible! Since I only had all of 30 minutes to do it. Some of the boys naturally got frustrated. "Misere man, when you gotta get some goggles yo! Ya keep feelin' on me man... that aint cool." So since I wasn't getting any sex, I started over achieving. I had enough damn awards to cover the whole left side of the cold murky walls in my basement room! Then I started buying porno magazines. And so my addiction to x-rated stuff started! But that's another story. Then one day, I decided to raise the bar. And this is where this story takes a French un-Catholic Caribbean twist!!!

I picked up one of my porn mags and saw this ad. It was this comic book like drawing of a very physically endowed male, I would find out just *how* endowed later on that day! The ad said "Sultry Boy." That and the picture was enough for this pent up sixteen year old! So I picked up the phone.

"Hello?" His voice growled and washed over me.

"A-a-allo?" I screeched like someone grabbed me by my religion.

"What can I do to you?" He sounded so casual, yet not cocky.

"Well, I was wondering what would you do for $30.00 bucks?" I was afraid he would hang up after that silly question. 'pleeease don't hang up, pleeeaase!' I thought.

"Well, what would you like to do?" Yesss! 'stay calm, don't blow this you horny little piss ass!' I gave myself a pep talk.

"I'm only sixteen, never done this before. So I only wanna kiss and hug and stuff." Oh what a chump I must have sounded like!

"That sounds good to me! Where do you live?" I drew a blank! A live breathing, testosterone pissing man had just agreed to come over me house! Oh joy! Now think...

"You know what, why don't I meet you at Forest Hills station to make it easier, that ok?" I lived in Hyde Park, Massachusetts then.

"Sure. Lets say 1 p.m?"

"Wait. What do you look like?"

"White male 6 feet blond blue, stocky build, 24." Everything he said was right except he looked 44 not 24 when we met! Which was all right by me since I'm into the "daddy" types.

"And what do **you** look like?"

"Well, I'm a black male, brown skinned black hair trim build, 5'11", and I'll be wearing a grey spring jacket with matching sunglasses."

"Great, I'll be carrying a green gym bag."

"Great! See ya then!" I said excitedly!

"Ya see ya."

click.

When we finally met at the train station, the afternoon heat was just climacteric. We both got there half an hour early. Apparently, I wasn't the only one eager and cocked with anticipation. I shook his hands and they felt like bricklayer hands, my knees quivered my loins panted like a runner! He had a white smile, for a white man. His hair was thinning and sun streaked. He had a few mature wrinkles around his eyes, particularly when he smiled, and he did not exude the same sexuality he exuded over the phone. In person, he seemed pitiable and unresponsive. But I didn't care. I took the big goon home!

I took him up to my parent's bedroom of all places! Being as big as he was, I figured we'd need a much bigger bed than mines. He wasted no time getting undressed. However, I did tell him that I would not take off my shirt or underwear. From what I learned from my mother and catholic school, one is to stay a virgin until marriage. However, how this applied to me, I didn't know. I was embarrassed at having to tell him that, but he just smiled it off. What he revealed underneath his clothes was a wet dream come true! A one-piece spandex-wrestling outfit!! Was this my lucky day or what? I sat on the edge of the bed, and he stood in front of me, his pelvic was at my eye level. What protruded from that was the biggest mound of flesh I've ever seen on any man! To the point where I foolishly asked him "what's that?" Duhhh! Then he bounded on top of me. "Kiss me!" I ordered him. He planted the biggest head on collision kiss on me ever! I mean seriously, it was like two trucks smashing face to face at full speed! "alright alright! no more kissing!" I begged him. "Let's just wrestle." As we continued to roll around in the bed, I was becoming more and more disappointed with this fantasy? Some how, I expected more, know what I mean? Then without warning, the situation **did** become more than I could handle when, *guess what*? Yep! My parents were coming home unexpectedly from work! Aaaahhh!!! I mean you see this stuff in movies, but you never imagine it happening to you for *real*! "Get dressed!!" I tried not to panic.

"Why what's going on?" He had this vacant look on his face. "Just get dressed, please?"

"It's my parents. They are coming up the stairs as we speak!" He muttered this "oh shit" sound and proceeded to dress. He was done in all of a minute! I on the other hand did not have time to button my pants when my mom bulldozed down the door! She found Sultry Boy on the recliner and all my books and me on the floor with my book bag opened spread out assimilating doing some homework.

"Hi!" She said in a psycho suspicious serial mom sort of way.

"Oh hi mom, dad. This is Mr. Sultry, he's my urrr...English tutor from school." I said like I was trying to convince myself.

"Uh....huh. Well, if you'll excuse me Mr. Sultry, I'm about to prepared dinner." And with that, I proceeded to take Mr. Sultry, I mean Sultry Boy down stairs. I couldn't help but feel cheated though. I mean I only got to spend an hour with him. I guess looking back, I should have been satisfied, but I wasn't. I figured that since my ass was toast anyways, hell I might as well get my money's worth! So when I got down stairs, I made him pinned me against the back porch wall. The hottest frottage EVER! I told him to grind his brute torso against me, all the while intertwining his bricklayer fingers with mines. And just when I was really getting into it...

"Miserrrre!" Shit, my mom was calling me. I fixed my clothes all the while gazing, beseeching him like a morose parched puppy in need of water. Then I took the final leap!

"Would you be my boyfriend?" I was so young.

"You wanna be boyfriends now?" He was obviously amused.

"Sure, why not?"

"Well, we'll see." and the last thing I heard was the door slamming behind him. I felt foolish for having asked the question only minutes after he left. I thought that I was probably going to be the laughing stock among his hooker friends. I was probably a joke to him. But all that had to wait because I still had to face my parents.

Mom was waiting for me in the master bedroom. Dad was watching TV, trying not to "make a big deal" of things, as he often puts it.

"Misere, now talk to your mother, that man was no tutor, was he?" I could see her eyes dancing around in her head, searching, beseeching for the truth.

"No mom, he wasn't." It was time to stop the hiding.

"Well, then? What was he?"

"I hired him from an adult magazine." The whole time, I was staring down at the floor.

"You like that kind of thing?" She was calm and very matter of fact with her demeanor.

"Yeah..." I was still looking down.

"Why? Is it something I did? Was I too tolerant? Too domineering perhaps?"

"No mom. You were a great mom, really." I finally looked up to meet her lustrous eyes.

"Then what then? How long have you felt this way?" her lips were starting to look pale.

"Since I was in first grade." I wanted desperately to free her from her guilt. But how could I free her from **her** guilt, when I wasn't even close to freeing **myself** from mines.

"Well let's put this matter to bed for a while. Don't tell your father a thing. Just promise me that you won't try this stuff again, here?"

"Yes, mama."

And that was that. I was left to wonder why this all happened. This whole thing reminded me of Pucks' soliloquy at the end of Shakespeare's A *Midsummer Night's Dream*: "...if these shadows have offended, think but this and all is mended, we have all but slumbered here, while these visions did appear, and this weak and idle theme, no more yielding then a dream." Except for me it wasn't a dream. It was my *reality*!

When I picked up that phone to call that "call boy", I didn't realize that it was going to change my life forever. But maybe my higher power knew that I was just about ready to embark on this journey that permeates my life 'til this day. This was *my* test. And I don't truly believe that this was the kind of test I could either past or fail. Just simply feeling ready to take this test was sufficient.

Pyramids of Truth

Josita Jones, being the diva that she think she is, sashes down Gullivan Boulevard, known as the Boulevard of broken dreams, in a tight short strapless red dress with white pumps, her hair done up in a bun, her lips painted with bright red lipstick and wearing Jackie O sunglasses. It does not take long for a red convertible to pull up alongside her. A man, who appears to be in his forties, ducks his head to accost her.

"Hi there... Can I give you a ride?" He asks with a smile on his face.

"Sure sugar. My feet are killing me in these hills," Josita says as she scrunches body into the car. "Now tell me what you *really* want." She gets right to the point. The man smiles nervously, look down then looks to the right at Josita. "Well, I'm going through a divorce right now, and I could use a little bit of a distraction," he says in an earnest tone. Josita smiles while shaking her head sideways. "I knew it," she says. "All you guys are the same. Always upta somethin'. Well, what do you have in mind sugar?" She says while batting her eyelashes playfully.

"Well, why don't we start with a blow job," says the man. Josita face expresses bemusement.

"Right here? On the boulevard?"

"Of course not," says the man. "Why don't we go somewhere a bit more isolated?"

"Hold it Romeo. That'll be fifty bucks upfront." Josita puts out her hand. The man reaches for his wallet and counts two twenties and a ten into her hand, then drives off...

"So, why are you divorcing your wife anyways?" Josita asks while she looks to her right out to the open fields decorated with nature's glorious wonders: steep dark and mysterious mountains, deep green grass swaying in the wind and the glaring sun napping on her face. She closes her eyes and takes it all in.

"I'm not divorcing her. She's divorcing me." The man says while looking straight ahead.

"Well, what's wrong with ya? Did she catch you cheatin' on her or somethin'? Josita continues to stare out the window, all the while munching on a piece gum and occasionally popping it.

"Or something," says the man with a stoic look on his face. "Well, we're here," he says.

"Where is this place anyways?" Josita asks while scanning her surroundings. The sun has just began to set in the belly of North Carolina's Smokey Mountains.

"It's called Lake Junaluska," responds the man. "Isn't it beautiful?"

"It sure is..." Josita trails her words as she continues to look around and then says, "Well? Are we gonna get down to business?" She looks over at the man. The man looks off into the distance as if transfixed by something obviously not visible to Josita.

"Not yet. Why don't we sit here a while. Enjoy the view," he says while still looking straight ahead.

"It's your money," she says as she walks over and sits down next to the man, takes off her shoes and hugs her knees to her chest. They both remain quiet for a while just looking around and listening to the chirping of birds and the streaming of the lake. After a while the man broke the silence. "You know," he begins while still looking into the distance. "I never thought it would turn out like this," he says while staring straight ahead, his eyes still transfixed as if he is somewhere else.

"Turn out like what?" Josita looks to her left at him.

"It seems like only yesterday I was graduating high school with my whole life ahead of me." Josita looks as if puzzled by the man's melancholy. "What do you have to complaint about? You're an upper middle class white male with a house with a white picket fence in the suburbs and you drive a Mercedes. You're living what most people would kill for. You're living the American Dream baby. And that's the truth," Josita ends her statement by accentuating the word "truth." The man is twirling a stick in the dirt. He sees a shiny white piece of rock. He digs a big hole in the dirt, pushes the rock down with his big bare hands and then buries it under the dirt. Then still looking off into the distance begins to talk.

"So to you its looks like I'm living the dream, eh?"

"Sure. Aren't you?"

"For some, what looks like the American dream can quickly become The American nightmare. I married my high school sweetheart right out of college and before you know, I got stuck with a job I didn't like while my wife stayed home to care for our two sons and life for me quickly became a monotonous routine and I found myself getting heart palpitations on Monday mornings just before I go to that wretched job. My wife and I slowly drifted apart and I started feeling just as much anxiety just before work, if not more so, whenever it was time for me to go home. We'er in debt up to our necks trying to keep up appearances and to top it off, my wife and I stopped having sex after the boys were born. Now, does that sound like the American dream to you?" Josita pops her gum, looks at the man while trying to mask the compassion she feels for him by seeming indifferent. "Well, if you put it that way, no, it doesn't," she says and quickly looks away.

"What about you? How did you end up doing...what you... do?" the man asks with hesitation in his voice. "Doing what I do? I know what you're thinking. I know you're judging me just like the rest of society. You probably think that I do this because I'm lazy, that I'd rather do this than get a 'real' job. For your information, I come from a wealthy family. They threw me out when they found out something about me that didn't fit their blue blood bullshit façade. I never even got to finish high school. I've been on my own since I was sixteen and that's when I started whoring. I even had a pimp for a while but he used to beat the shit out of me and steal my money. I've had three abortions because I don't think I'm fit to ever be a real mother to a kid and I don't ever want to be like my asshole parents, ever! Life for me is day to day survival. I even tried to go straight and tried to get a 'real' job, but no one wants to hire a high school dropout. And even I wanted to go back to school, how would I support myself? I'm used to well of white man like you looking down your noses at me and that's the truth. But none of you know me. So you all can kiss my whorish black ass!" At this point her voice is shaking with emotion that she is trying so very hard to hold back and her sunglasses hide her eyes that have begun to tear up. The man reaches out and tries to touch her hands but she quickly pulls them away.

"Hey I don't need your pity, ok?" She says facing the man.

"I was just trying to...I mean, I just want you to know that I understand." The man looks away as he too begins to tear up. By this time, the sun has been swallowed by the North Carolina Mountains completely and they both now sit in pitch black darkness. The only sounds audible are the sounds of their breaths and the crickets. Josita looks over to see the man shoulders begins to heave up and down and then he stopped coving his mouth and begins to sob uncontrollably; it's as if every painful emotion he'd ever felt have suddenly swept like a storm over his body. Josita puts her hands on his shoulders.

"Hey hey. Its ok sweetie"

"No its not!" says the man through his sobs. "I don't think you understand me at all...No one does!" The man—now feeling a completeness of grief, hopelessness, desire and pain—sobs increasingly louder. "Can you just hold me for a while?" He asks in a low child like voice. Josita hesitates, and then she reluctantly says in a very deep brassy voice, "I'm... ..I'm really a man you know." She braces herself for a volcanic expression of disgust from the man. But none was forth coming. Then ever so softly, the man says "I know. That's why I picked you up." Now blanketed by the night, the moon hovers over them like a halo as they hold each other. They both dread returning to their respective places in life: the man back to his suburban home life and Josita to the Boulevard of broken dreams. But right here, right now, in this tender moment, they had each other and that's all that really matters.

Nemesis

Once during the time of the Genesis of all living things and beings on earth, God created Adam and Steve. They were two statuesque paragons of the male form.

The first male was a tall White male with shoulder length silky blond hair that glowed and shimmered like gold under the sun. He was not too densely muscular, with eyes as blue as the blue of the clear blue sky and even bluer then the azure sea. He had full red lips, long eyelashes and smooth radiant skin. God named him Adam.

The second male was yet another tall male, but of a different shade than Adam. His skin was a deep dark purple color, a buxom shining example of African superior musculature and regal splendor akin to a textbook illustration of the male anatomy and physique. He possessed a baldhead so glossy it reflected the skies above; with chiseled cheeks and a broad milky white smile made even whiter by his darker skin color. God named him Steve.

Unbeknownst to them, they were both nude as they wandered about in the forest that was budding with new life and grandeur, beauty and color. In the distance there was a nearby river. God told Adam and Steve *not* to frolic in the water and they obeyed for some time.

Most of their days were spent wondering in and around the forest picking flowers, eating the vegetation, chasing butterflies during the day and catching fireflies at night. They often played games like "hide and go seek", "catch me if you can" and "I dare you to take me down my friend"; the last one being Steve's personal favorite because of his perceived superior strength and musculature.

During the evening hours, they lay down together under the shelter of a Weeping Willow, they were on their backs and so their eyes were watching God, the moon and stars that hovered above them somberly, as if sensing the presence of an imminent catastrophe. They would tell each other fables and since their minds hadn't any previous memory, in essence was a "tabula rasa" or blank slate, they made up the parables as they went along keeping one another joyful and blissful; not knowing that in their near future there laid sorrow.

There was one allegory that particularly stood out in Steve's memory and he requested that Adam tell it to him again. That night, the moon hung so low above them that they thought that they could quite possibly reach out and tap its creamy surface. Adam's White skin made even whiter as he retells Steve the allegory and Steve's dark skin made even darker by the milky moon glow as he listened intently.

"Once upon a time, there was this drifter who was floating along in life like a leaf in the windy weather. Before he began his journey, God told him that he would come upon a male statue in the deep of the forest and he was *not* to touch it under any circumstances.

Then one day, he came upon this daring looking male statue, and was fascinated by this Greek God like sculpture thinking that he was probably a deity of some sort. The sculpture was imbued with extraordinary aesthetic sensibilities. It produced light like "art" in motion; some sort of scientific solace regarding the sound of his skin like a first meeting with an eccentric enthusiast. He was utterly enchanted and he felt paralyzed by it, so much so that he knew that he had to touch it. He then raised his hands; which trembled with the knowledge that he was committing a major error in judgment. He then grazed the sinewy physique of this ancient God like sculpture and winced as his fingers lingered on the spectacularly detailed musculature and grandeur of the God like sculpture. The sculpture, whose image possessed a somber reverent quality eventually, opened his eyes; which were engulfed in fire! Then slowly and deliberately the rest of the sculpture became swallowed up in flames; fantastic jarring colors, blue, red, orange and yellow! Then, with parted fiery lips uttered in a voice that shook the ground awake like an approaching earthquake! He said, "You dare to touch me, mate? You shall then perish and meet a somber fate!" After which his head suddenly fell off and became a rolling ball of fire! The rest of him, now also in flames that rose higher and higher until the storm clouds broke and there came a ferocious shower of fire! The offending drifter started running and wailing, his arms flailing and his cries piercing until he lost his voice completely and eventually dissipated and all that was left of him was a minute pile of ashes. The earth was calm and peaceful once again. The End."

"Wow," said Steve. "That was quite a story! Can you tell it to me again, so that I can commit it to memory?" Steve beseeched

"No. Maybe tomorrow. I'm tired and I think we both need to get to sleep." And with that, Steve spooned Adam and they both fell asleep sheathed in each other's arms.

The next day, the supple hands of nature caressed their cheeks like a loving mother, awaking them to greet the new day, which like a "tabula rasa" or blank slate, waited to be written upon. The breath of the earth twirled across their eyes so that they could see better, then slowly collapsed like a graceful silhouette as the dirge of songs birds echoed in the distance. The heat that day was particularly aggressive and oppressive. The midday sun stood nude, electrifying the panting breaths of "want" emanating from Adam and Steve and what they "wanted" was to cool off or risk dying of heat exhaustion. Then all of a sudden, they heard this booming voice like rolling thunder declaring, "I am God. Put your faith in my hands and you will want for nothing." And they obeyed for some time.

The intensity of the heat was worsening and Adam and Steve were by this time panting like dogs and rivulets of sweat started to sting their eyes to the point where they could barely see. Then with a sudden scream of exasperation, they bolted towards the river in unison to the ear piercing sounds of rolling thunder! They were frolicking in the water like children at the onset of recess and recreation, riding heat waves into oblivion, humming a tune only a crow could bite into—the crow is said to be an emblem of pending death and there were a few waiting and milling around patiently by the river.

Gradually, they began to become aware of their nudity, which rendered them both embarrassed and aroused simultaneously. They then began to approach each other to consummate their desire as the water, which appeared deceptively docile caressed their sexually charged bodies. Then suddenly, the water turned into a tumultuous eddying mass, a violent current that threatened to pull them down below the surface! Furthermore and to their horror, their arms and legs began to feel anesthetized, as they tried to escape the wrath of the river! Their arms and legs steadily lost all feeling altogether and they began to sink down under! As they went down below the surface of the river, they stared at each other, their eyes expressing regret but otherwise possessed a calm resolve as they disappeared altogether under the water. The earth was calm and peaceful once again.

Midnight in Utopia

J ust before Jean-Louis straddles his bike on his way home from the gym, he checks his cell phone for the time since he's going out tonight. The autumn night air whistles and dances anxiously around him. He is thinking about how lonely he's been and how marvelous it would be to meet someone tonight. He is not fastidious about whom and thinks maybe he should be. He is in love with love and every year he hopes that, like the autumn leaves, his luck will change.

He grew-up in Haiti. His mother was like a fading flower, trapped in a loveless marriage of convenience to his dad. Both were stern and never really told him they loved him no matter how hard he tried to please them. He left Haiti twenty years ago to start a new life in America, where his search for identity and love continues to intensify.

Now he lives as a gay man in Boston. But he soon learns that the gay lifestyle comes with a price and quickly becomes a harrowing experience. He is aware that "hot" in this gay Mecca, means that one must have the perfect job, perfect body, perfect teeth, live in an ideal neighborhood, and be perpetually 29 or under to be part of the "A list crowd." He, however, is an under paid bank teller with an average body, living in a dilapidated and dangerous part of Dorchester and he's 40. But at least he has good teeth.

So he looks forward to Utopia, a gay bar in Cambridge. His friends often joke that the place should have been called "Parasites." He gets there by midnight, takes a sharp inrush of breath and goes through the door and straight to the dance floor hoping to be noticed. There, he observes the usual myriad of muscle boys with bare chests posing, drinks in hand and laden with a strange combination of insecurity and arrogance.

On the dance floor, he dances freely and intensely, as if he is trying to shake off all of his neuroses about not feeling good enough. But although his feet are burning up, he feels hollow inside, like a deep dark well of nothingness. This feeling almost overtakes him and he feels like crying. But not here, not now, he thinks to himself. As he relinquishes himself to the music, he wonders if the brawny blonde in the crowd of clones is staring at him. Thinking this notion implausible. But the blonde smiles at him enticingly. So he dances his way towards him, extend his hand and pulls him to the dance floor.

"What's your name?" He yells, still in disbelief of his luck.

"Shawn, and you?" Blondie yells back, displaying perfect white teeth.

"Jean-Louis. Nice to meetcha."

"Same here. So are you French?"

"Oui, Haitian French." Soon Shawn starts to grind his perfectly round derriere against Jean-Louis's mounting crotch and he responds by grabbing Shawn by the waist, pulling him hard against his pelvic. Jean-Louis then turns Shawn around to face him, his chest panting with anticipation. He then grasps Shawn by the head and squashes his lips onto him with quick frenzied kisses.

"Hey slow down dude. So, what are you into?" asks Shawn.

"Well, I tend to be a little conservative when it comes to sex. To me sex is only good when your heart is in it. I like to take things slow, you know. Courting to me is the ultimate high. I lo-"

"I love Haiti." Shawn interrupts. "Haitian men are such voracious fuckers. I can't tell you how many times I've been fucked silly, I-"

"You say you love Haiti. Have you ever been there?" Jean-Louis asks with some annoyance and suspicion as Shawn's words snuffs his enthusiasm.

"No, but I've been with lots of Haitian men." Shawn says with a hint of a smirk on his face. "So, how big is that Haitian Co"-

"A gentleman never tells. If we go on a date…then maybe…"

"Hey, listen. I don't date." Shawn snaps back, suddenly sneering. "I do one merci fuck a year and tonight, you were it since you were so desperate for my attention. So I thought I'd throw you a bone, a big one too if you'd kept your mouth shut! Did you really think that a guy like me could love a troll like you?" He hisses as he disappears into the crowd, leaving Jean-Louis in a speechless stupor. Shawn's words come to him with cannon like force. He feels a shapeless horror rising inside of him, like a current threatening to drown him. He never saw Shawn again for the rest of the night, or since. One night in Utopia, he sees a guy with a T-shirt that reads, "I'm lost. Can you please take me home?" The pathetic desperation in the guy's eyes both scared and angered him. That night, he left the bar with tears flooding down his face.

***

He stopped going to Utopia after that night. Instead, he decides to rediscover his love of reading, particularly this book ubiquitous among gay men and aptly titled "Finding the Boyfriend Within." He also joins a gay friendly Church, volunteers and just enjoys the company of his friends and family.

His aura now communicates a new sense of pride and purpose, thankful that the capricious club scene is now behind him. Then one sunny Sunday in Church just around noon, he suddenly recognizes an internal alarm of the series of events that had preceded his new life. He smiles in nostalgic demarcation of his past and present. And then *He* came. While sitting in the Church pew, he looks up to see this dashingly dressed man towering over him with a coy smile. "Excuse me", he says. "But, is this seat taken?" His voice caressed his ears like the fingers of warm honey. He scoots over with exaggerated zeal and says, "No, not at all. Not-at-all…"

The Purloined Heart

Lonely people often have a story that they feel compelled to tell. That was the case with Victor DeMargo. I was sitting at the 1369 Coffee House at Inman Sq. in Cambridge, where I often enjoy my daily cup of Chai Tea and the local artist types that drop in and out throughout the day. I don't particularly care for corporate mega chain establishments like Starbucks, since they make it their mission to put Mom and Pop type places out of business. Domination. That's all it is. The whole world is about domination and control. And if you don't agree with me, then you must be delusional.

So anyways, I was sitting at my usual table in the far corner in the back near the bathroom, that way I can observe the myriad of Cambridge eccentrics that float in and out of the place. Then he walked in. A tall slender White male with sharp facial features, particularly his protruding nose and chiseled cheek bones. Even though he was clean shaven, his mustache looked like it had been plucked right off his upper lips. He looked like a man with a story to tell. We made eye contact while he was in line and he then made his way to the back and asked if he could join me.

I usually prefer to be alone but he compelled a curiosity in me that was relentless. I had to find out what his story was. I could never resist a man with a good story. It must stem from growing up in Haiti, where every night during blackouts, the whole family would gather on our front porch while our grandmother—who was known to spike her tea with a few drops of whisky—would regale us with colorful tales by moonlight. That is the one thing from my childhood that doesn't make me cringe when I remember. And so now, as a middle aged man, whenever I yearn to re-connect with my youth, I seek to hear a story from anyone with a story to tell.

I have been to hear Brother Blue, a local legend and master story teller many a times right here in Cambridge. When you hear his stories, you almost feel like you're tripping on LSD or something to that effect. He once described how God made the world by sneezing out the animals, sneezing out the trees and sneezing out a motley crew of humans. Anyways, back to the stranger with a story. He told me his name was Victor DeMargo and he just moved here from Portland, Oregon. Then he started speaking on the subject of love.

"What is Love?" He asked and I could tell by his manner that the question was rhetorical. "Love, love, love. That elusive feeling of the ultimate form of adoration can quickly morph into desperation and destruction in every sense of the word. How do you explain how one can both love and hate someone at the same time? How can you explain the reasons why you love someone? Love is a selfish feeling. It can hold the participants hostage. It can drive one to kill, steal and commit unspeakable acts." I just sat there; tapping my finger tips on the table, trying to hear what he *wasn't* saying and wondering when he would get on with it. *Tell me the god damn story already* was what I wanted to say. But I decided to utilize the virtue of patience. Besides, I had nothing else better to do.

"Love is elusive. But it's even more elusive when it's between two men. Now I'm not talking about the love two gay men can share. I'm talking about love between a heterosexual man and a homosexual man. Is that possible you ask? Yes, most definitely. I once knew this guy, let's call him Joey Defalco since I prefer not to use his real name. So Joey Defalco fell in love in the men's locker room at Bally's Total Fitness in Porter Square. When he first laid eyes on Clark Bent, a paragon of male beauty and masculinity at six feet 5 inches tall and a heavily muscled smooth Black body, wearing jockstraps that left little to the imagination and a fluorescent smile that probably glows in the dark, he thought that he has just discovered the meaning of life and the reason why he was born. Joey Defalco just stood there; gawking and contemplating professing his undying love right there amidst a line-up of swinging willies and exposed derrieres. Clark Bent, as he was rising from tying his shoes, caught Joey Defalco gawking at him and with a sly smile said "Hi there. Had a good work-out?" Joey Defalco opened his mouth to respond but nothing was forthcoming. It was as if he had suddenly swallowed his own tongue. "I'm Clark Bent and… you are?" He finally found his voice again, "Joey. Joey Defalco."

"Well nice to meet you Joey. Joey Defalco. So did you have a good work-out?" Clark Bent beamed his ultra white smile as he makes small talk with Joey Defalco, who could not bring himself to look directly at Clark Bent since he felt the beginnings of a sudden swelling in his crotch area; which he tried to hide unsuccessfully with a towel wrapped tightly around his waist. Clark Bent glanced quickly at Joey Defalco's crotch area and averted his eyes so not to make Joey Defalco feel any more embarrassment than he was already feeling. He finished getting dressed and said "Well Joey Defalco, I hope to see you here again sometime" and quickly left the locker-room before Joey Defalco could say anything back.

Well, from that point on, Joey Defalco could not stop thinking about Clark Bent. He thought about him when he went to bed at night and when he got up in the morning. He thought about him while brushing his teeth, during breakfast, at work and again when he got home. He went to the gym everyday around the same time hoping to see Clark Bent again, and this time he knew he would not act like such a tongue tied little horny queen who suddenly pitched a tent in Clark Bent's presence. And then it happened. Clark Bent was just getting in just as Joey Defalco was changing into his workout clothes.

"Hey it's Joey Defalco. Well, well. It's nice to see you again!" Clark Bent said with surprising elation in his voice and his eyes were moist and wide with excitement. *Keep it together Defalco. Try not to make a fool of yourself*, Joey Defalco silently said to himself. "Nice to to see see you too Clark Bent." And then Clark Bent said, "Hey, I have an idea. Why don't we work out together? I mean, if you wouldn't mind?" Joey Defalco felt a surge of electricity running through his veins and for a moment felt as if the whole interaction was surreal. He just could not believe his luck!

"Sure. I'd li- like that ver-very mu-much" he could barely get the words out. Then as Clark Bent stood over Joey Defalco while he was bench pressing, he proceeded to talk about his beautiful wife Delfina Bigbresta, a blond hair blue eyed gal from Poland. He talked about how they met on the internet and have been together for 2 years and married for 1. At that moment, Joey Defalco's felt his heart plummet like a brick to the bottom of the sea. He felt that all hope was lost at any chance of coupling with Clark Bent. But he hid his feelings by acting obsequious about Clark Bent mention of his beloved wife, "Wow! Congratulations! Sounds like you are one lucky man. You must bear the envy of every man who sees you with her!" And Clark Bent just smiles and says "Yeah, I really am. How about you? Do you have someone special?" Joey Defalco did not anticipate that question and again felt tongue tied. "Well, not yet… but I'm hoping." Afterwards, they exchanged phone numbers and Clark Bent told Joey Defalco that he will be calling him soon to maybe play basketball together. Joey Defalco, who has absolutely no interest in basketball, said "Sure. I'd love to. I lo-love basketball. It's my favorite sport!" *Liar*! He said to himself but he would even agree to go bungee jumping just to be in the presence of Clark Bent.

The late afternoon sun hung like an orange on the Far East side of the sky as they play basketball together. There was no one else on the court and there was a quiet intensity in the air as if there was an impending thunder storm nearing. It became obvious to Clark Bent that Joey Defalco did not know how to play basketball. So Clark Bent got behind Joey Defalco and with his big muscular hands over Joey Defalco's, tried to show him how to get the ball into the hoop. At this point, Joey Defalco was shaking like a leaf in the rain and Clark Bent put his lips next to his ears and whispered in a very wet soothing yet bass filled voice "Relax…take a deep breath and shoot." And Joey Defalco almost did just that, except it wasn't the basketball.

They continued to do things together over the next few months and one day Clark Bent invited Joey Defalco over for dinner so that he could meet his wife. Something Joey Defalco wasn't particularly looking forward to, but he sucked it up and acted eager and grateful for the invite.

When Joey Defalco first layed eyes on Delfina Bigbresta Bent, he thought she looked like a porcelain statuette with long straight blond hair, high sleek cheek bones and blue eyes, an hourglass figure and young. Very very young. She must be no older than 21 years old with breast that resembled oversized coconut like orbs of dancing loveliness and Joey thought "How could I possibly compete with that?" But for Clark Bent's sake, he met her and made pleasantries all the while looking at his watch anticipating the end of the evening.

As time went by, Joey Defalco and Clark Bent developed a routine of hanging out together every Friday night at the local bar to drink and play pool together. And each time, they grew closer and closer. Clark Bent started to confide in Joey Defalco about his relationship with his wife. He told him that all is not as perfect as it seems and that he has certain "feelings" that he feels he can't talk Delfina about. That they've stopped communicating and being each other's best friends and confident ever since they had their son, Clark Bent Jr. Clark Bent did not anticipate them growing apart so swiftly. Joey Defalco tried desperately to appear empathetic. He tried desperately to hide his joy over Clark Bent's discontentment with his home life because this clearly left the door wide open for him to infiltrate himself into their lives and push their already troubled relationship over the edge. *Home wrecker! I am nothing but a little horny home wrecker!* Joey Defalco thought to himself. Joey Delfalco was more than elated to allow Clark Bent to bend his ears with his problems with Delfina and it didn't take long for them spend even more time together when all of a sudden, Joey Defalco suggested that they go away to Cape Cod for an entire weekend.

This was to be his moment of truth: the seduction of Clark Bent. Clark Bent told Delfina that he and Joey Defalco were going "fishing" together on the cape, since that's what Joey Defalco told him. Little did he know that Joey Defalco had reserved a hotel room with just one Queen sized bed.

He was in for a surprise once he got there. By this point, Clark Bent have grown closer to Joey Defalco emotionally so that he didn't feel uncomfortable in his presence, even though he was aware of Joey Defalco's sexual attraction to him, something he chose to ignore since it did not pose any immediate threat to his own sexuality. As a matter of fact, the whole scenario was a welcomed distraction from his unsatisfactory home life since he and Delfina stopped having sex as regularly as it was in the beginning. Their life had become a dreaded monotony of predictable routine. And Joey Defalco presented an opportunity for excitement, mystery and suspense. The stuff that great novels are made of with Clark Bent as the handsome protagonist with the potential to be a heartbreaker.

When they got to the Heritage House Hotel in Hyannis, they checked in and upon entering the room, Clark Bent noticed for the first time that there was only one bed. He looked coyly at Joey Defalco while shaking his head from side to side and Joey Defalco just smiled with a hint of sparkle in his eyes. That night, after spending time walking on Main Street window shopping and visiting the JFK museum, they stripped down to their bathing suits and went to the pool area which had a hot tub and sauna. Joey Defalco got to see Clark Bent in a tiny tightly stretched Speedo that left little to the imagination and the blood inside his own swimming trunk got all upset and he could not hide the embarrassing swelling growing in his pelvic area, which he tried to hide by staying under the water in the hot tube until he felt safe to come back up.

He began to think about their sleeping arrangement for later. What if Clark Bent slept with his back to him? That would be humiliating and he was not sure that he could handle that. But later, as the sun went down and the sky turned a reddish orange, they finally went to bed, and Clark Bent emerged from the bathroom completely naked and Joey Defalco breathed a sigh of relief and pulled back the covers and took Clark Bent into his arms, his heart grinning and blushing with pleasure and excitement. Outside, the moon hovered by their window creating a luminescent glow highlighting their unspoken feelings for one another and Joey Defalco wished he could freeze time and so that they could stay like this forever. All they did during the nights was holding each other without even words in-between their hard naked bodies. It was the purest kind of love, akin to the slow burning love between virginal teenagers; as innocent as fresh running water in a remote mountain stream, unsoiled by human presence. But soon, he knew that Clark Bent would have to go back to his beautiful wife in his beautiful home in Cambridge. *Something must be done about the wife*, he thought. He was never one to believe in Voodoo, but this was an extreme case, he could not go on living if he could not be with Clark Bent. So he decided to consult with his Father, who when he was in Haiti, was an Ougan which means a Voodoo priest with magical powers.

He told his father about his relationship with Clark Bent. His father was not completely thrilled about his son being gay, but he loved him nevertheless and he wanted to do whatever he could to help his son. He told his dad that he wanted Clark Bent to fall out of love with Delfina and completely in love with him. He wanted Clark Bent's love to be so fixated on himself that his heart would love no one else except him and him only until the day he dies. His father warned him that there might be some danger in someone loving you to that kind of extreme but he would have none of it. He has never heard of someone dying from too much love and he begged his dad to prepare a spell so that he could cast it on Clark Bent. His father told him that he would have to steal a string of Clark Bent's hair and bring it back to him. With that, he would prepare the portion that would steal Clark Bent's love away from Delfina.

While Joey Defalco was visiting Clark Bent one day, and much to his contentment, Delfina was not home. Clark Bent was fixing lunch and Joey Defalco excused himself to go to the lavatory. Looking over his shoulders to make sure it was safe; he gently pushed the bathroom door open, tip toed in and stole a string of Clark Bent's hair from his hairbrush, put it in piece of napkin and stuck it in his pocket before making his way back to the kitchen. Later that afternoon, he brought the Ougan the string of hair. His dad told him that he would have the portion ready by the upcoming weekend, when he knew he would be spending time with Clark Bent.

Joey Defalco's father had prepared the love portion for him to use on Clark Bent by the next weekend as promised. The portion was in the same type of bottle genies come out of in fantasy movies. It was a blood colored liquid that the Ougan told Joey Defalco to put in Clark Bent's drink. Joey Defalco made plans to go camping with Clark Bent that same weekend and he felt anxious in anticipating the moment he will cast the love spell on him.

He remembered when he became sick when he was just seven years old, that his mother—who believed that he fell ill because he was under some evil spell of the local Ougan—who had been a friend of his family—for making fun of him. You see, the Ougan had these weird lips, his upper lip was much shorter than the lower and looked like as if it was turned inside out which caused his front teeth to be permanently exposed. One day while he was running by and the then 8 year old Joey Defalco—who was sitting on his front porch with cohorts he wanted to impress—called out "Hey, it's the man with the weird lips!" And all the kids cried out "Oooooohhhh…" and fell into a hush of fear and shock that Joey Defalco would dare insult the most feared man in the neighborhood. The Ougan looked over at Joey Defalco and said "Oke Ti pi tit mwouin," which is creole for "O.k. my son." Feeling consumed by fear and regret, Joey Defalco confided in his dad about what the Ougan said and to his horror, his dad told him that when the Houngan used the words "My son" that meant quite literally that he now possessed Joey Defalco's soul. And so later that day, his dad went to the Ougan and asked for a pardon for his son and to his relief, the pardon was granted.

Clark Bent picked up Joey Defalco for the camping trip on a Sunday afternoon at sun set. Some storm clouds were gathering in the mostly blue skies and the birds were scurrying around and chirping very loudly. Once Clark Bent reached the highway and with his eyes still on the road, he reached over for Joey Defalco's hand and gave it a tight squeeze before letting go and putting his hand back on the wheel. Joey Defalco felt a rush of guilt and pleasure; the guilt due to his pending sorcerer like trick on Clark Bent. Fearing that his eyes would give him away, he looked away from Clark Bent to stare out the window and out into the open fields of deep green trees and bushes rushing by as the mountains, with mouths seemingly wide open, began to swallow the evening sun. His thoughts were flashing by as fast as the trees themselves. He started thinking about how he would execute his plan. In order to mask the portion, he brought the ingredients to make "sex on the beach," a drink that is already reddish in color.

Later, that evening, they sat by the fire roasting marshmallows and Joey Defalco decided to break the silence and engage Clark Bent in conversation.

"So…how does it feel to be married?" He asked with his eyes transfixed on the flickering fire, which was yellowish orange with a tinge of occasional blue, creating shadows that danced around their mysterious surroundings.

"It's alright, I guess. It's a little different than what I expected," said Clark Bent and he too still stared at the fire.

"Well what did you expect?" Joey Defalco looked over at Clark Bent with furrowed brows.

"I suppose I thought that the honeymoon stage would last at least five years or so. But as it turned out, it's more like five months. Maybe we shoulda waited on having the kid and all."

Now surrounded by night and shadows, the sounds of crickets chirping all seem to accentuate nature's presence. He looked up to see the moon hovering seemingly directly over Clark Bent's head creating the illusion of a halo. He opened his mouth to say something to Clark Bent but then changed his mind, not wanting to spoil the moment by making some silly nelly emotional confession. He then began to take furtive glances at Clark Bent until he could no longer help himself and just surrendered to completely ogling him. Clark Bent still staring at the fire began to say "I…I…" but could not complete his sentence. Joey Defalco was starting to feel antsy as he began to think about how he was going to taint Clark Bent's drink. He almost changed his mind when he looked over and saw how angelic Clark Bent looked by the firelight gleaming on his face, almost making him look like a glowing half smiling Halloween pumpkin. But then he thought, "I've come this far, I might as well go through with it."

"Would you care to have a drink with me before we go to bed?"

"Sure, I don't see why not." And so Joey Defalco began to pour the drinks with his back to Clark Bent. He pulled the portion in a stealthy fashion and quickly poured it in Clark Bent's drink. He then turned around with a smile on his face and said, "There you are. Just what the doctor ordered." He poured his drink and joined Clark Bent in a toast. "To a long friendship and a long life," Joey Defalco said and Clark Bent said "Dido." Except for Clark Bent, his life would soon come to a gruesome end.

That night, they spooned together in complete silence, both pretending to sleep by keeping their eyes closed, but their thoughts were running amuck. What Clark Bent wasn't saying to Joey Defalco was: "I don't know nor do I understand what's going on here. I have these feelings for you, but yet I'm not gay. Even though we're going through a rough time right now, I love my wife and I'm not about to leave her for an uncertain future with you as some type of gay couple. But yet, I've fallen in love you. So what am I gonna do? This whole thing is so fucking confusing!"

What Joey Defalco was not saying to Clark Bent was: "I love you with all my heart and I'm convinced you love me too. I know you think you're straight, but you're not. I can tell by the way you look at me when you think I'm not looking, by the way you touch me and run your finger gently over my face, lips and down to my belly button, which you just love to play with. I know we have not gone all the way, but it's just a matter of time before you come to your senses and squirt your love inside of me and I will forever be there to receive you, over and over again."

About a week after that night, Clark Bent began to show signs that the portion was working. He began to spend every day with Joey Defalco and hardly ever went home to his wife after work. Delfina located Joey Defalco's phone number in Clark Bent's cell phone and began calling him and demanding that he tells Clark

Bent to come home to her. But Joey Defalco would just roll his eyes, mutter "Crazy Bitch" and just hang up on her. Clark Bent even began to go all the way with Joey Defalco. They were screwing each other regularly, sometimes four to five times a day. Clark Bent just couldn't seem to keep his hands off Joey Defalco. Sometimes, he would be cooking dinner, and Clark Bent would sneak up on him from behind, yank down his pants, throw him against the kitchen counter and just bang him until Joey screamed for him to stop while the next door neighbors would start banging on the walls. Some days, Joey Defalco could barely walk, when he did, he would do so slowly with his right hand turned back over his right butt cheek, all the while cursing Clark Bent under his breath with a bemused smile on his face. Little did he knew, that Clark Bent's excessive attention would eventually drive him to commit murder.

Clark Bent eventually filed for divorce from his wife and moved in with Joey Defalco. He refused to go to work because he wanted to spend all his time with Joey Defalco. He would follow him around everywhere. He could not even go to the bathroom without Clark Bent leaning on the opposite side of the door, trying to maintain a conversation with him until Joey Defalco was done. And when Joey Defalco had to go to work, Clark Bent would go into a fit and began crying and Joey Defalco would always end up being late for work since he had to console him. Then he started to go to work with Joey Defalco at the department store where he worked as a sales associate. He would hang around all day, feigning browsing as if he was a customer until it was time to take Joey Defalco home.

Clark Bent ended up proposing to Joey Defalco and eventually married him in a formal commitment ceremony in front of their friends and family. Clark Bent completely stopped working in a desperate effort to totally devote himself to Joey Defalco. He became quite literally a "Desperate House Fag", cooking, cleaning and waiting on Joey Defalco like a fawning eager to please puppy. At first, Joey Defalco thought "Great. The potion is working." But the more submissive Clark Bent was, the more infuriated and disenchanted Joey Defalco became. It was as if Clark Bent's personality and sense of identify had been completely purged by the potion. Clark Bent agreed with everything Joey Defalco said like a five year old frantically trying to please his father. Clark Bent's obsession even kept him from being with his friends and family.

Now feeling completely isolated and with his back against the wall, Joey Defalco had had enough. So he went back to his Ougan dad to request another potion to reverse that dreadful spell on Clark Bent. To his dismay, his father told him that the spell could not be undone and that he was condemned to be with Clark Bent until one of them died. And so that was when Joey Defalco made up his time to do the unthinkable: he resolved to kill Clark Bent.

It was a day like any other. Clark Bent was following Joey Defalco around the house as he was getting ready to go to work. Joey Defalco went about his business as if Clark Bent wasn't there at all. Just when he was ready to leave, Clark Bent commenced crying as usual and he hugged and consoled him, patting his back and saying "There, there. I'll be home soon enough." After Joey Defalco left, Clark Bent decided to go to the living room, sat in front of an 8x11 photograph of Joey Defalco, and just scrutinized it as if he was hypnotized by it. At times, he felt that the picture was scowling at him with furrowed eyebrows and squinty eyes. He remained there all day long, only leaving occasionally to go to the bathroom.

When Joey Defalco left work, he stopped by the hardware store to purchase some arsenic—which is a form of rat poison— to prepare Clark Bent's dinner. At the store, Joe the store owner smiled and asked him "Hey Joey, I see you're having pest problems, eh?" Joey Defalco avoided looking at Joe then immediately left the store to avoid any more probing questions. When you frequent mom and pop establishments like Joe's Hardware, the proprietor is so used to seeing you; he tends to importune into your personal life. Before you know it, gossip is not too far behind and he didn't want to raise any suspicion about his murderous intentions.

He put Clark Bent's arsenic laced clam chowder in a red bowl and his in a blue bowl so that he wouldn't eat from the wrong bowl by mistake. He had to be very stealthy since Clark Bent sat in the kitchen the whole time watching him cook, his eyes following Joey Defalco around like the eyes in a picture.

Days turned into months and Clark Bent refused to die. So Joey Defalco resolved to take a more drastic measure. It was a Sunday evening; he waited for Clark Bent to fall asleep. He then went into the kitchen, retrieved a knife big enough to slaughter a cow and proceeded to go into the bedroom. He skulked towards the bed and abruptly stopped when the floor board squeaked. Clark Bent turned to lie on his back. At the bedside, he hovered over Clark Bent raising the giant knife as high as he could, in the opposite wall; his oversized shadow was elongated so that the knife looked like it came from the ceiling. Just as he was bringing the knife down, Clark Bent suddenly opened his eyes, saw the knife and bellowed out continuous loud screeches as Joey Defalco stabbed him dead in the heart many times over until Clark Bent was forever silenced. He stabbed him so hard that the knife went straight through his chest cavity and out through his back, making a large slit in the bed sheet. Clark Bent's heart was squirting blood like an out of control sprinkler system. He quickly grabbed a heavy blanket and threw it over Clark Bent.

When the blood finally stopped, he dragged Clark Bent's body off the bed and it made a loud thud when it hit the floor. He then proceeded to pry open his chest with the giant knife, grabbed the lacerated heart with his bare hands and held it up to the ceiling and said: "Ougan, your curse have driven me to this, that I should take the life of the man I love. But I know God will forgive me and curse *you* to hell!" He decided that he would cook and eat the heart. He then brought the heart into the kitchen, placed it into a pot with a little bit of oil, and began to cook it, occasionally sprinkling spices onto it. While he let it simmer on low heat, he went into the bedroom, wrapped Clark Bent's body in multiple layers of sheets and dragged him to the back yard. He dug up a hole and dumped the body by rolling it away from himself.

When he got back to the house and as he was changing his bloody clothes, he heard some loud urgent pounding at the door. He peered into the peep hole.

"It's the police! Open up!" The voice sounded threatening and commanding. With trembling hands, and the beginning of beads of sweat streaking down on either side of his forehead, he reluctantly opened the door.

"Good evening, Sir. There has been a complaint from your neighbor about some suspicious activity taking place in this apartment."

"Whatever do you mean, officer?" He tried to look nonplused and completely free from culpability.

"Some high pitched screams were heard and then you were seen dragging something long wrapped up in sheets out to the back yard." The officer said as he tried to look around and over Joey Defalco's shoulders. "Do you mind if I take a look around?" Joey Defalco felt a surge of panic creeping up his throat like undigested food. He had to think of something quick, since the entire bedroom was still covered with blood stains everywhere. And will all the nonchalance he could muster, he said, "Well officer, I was just preparing dinner. It's been a long day and so I'm famished. Hey, I know this is unusual, but would you care to join me?" The officer looked at him with bewilderment in his eyes. Then he smiled and said, "Sure, why not. I skipped lunch today since we've been so busy. There's been a lot of homicides in the city lately. What's this world coming to?" He then stepped inside with his hands hanging over his gun belt.

Joey Defalco served him a salad along with a generous helping of Clark Bent's heart before they sat down to dinner together. "This is the best meat I've ever tasted! I'd love to have the recipe to give to my wife." Joey Defalco snickered while looking at him and said, "Do you really?" Then he said to himself, "What a good looking guy. Surely the most handsome cop I've ever seen. I wonder if he likes to play basketball."

***

As Victor De Marco got up to leave, I swiftly placed my hands over his and asked "Whatever happened to Joey Defalco?" He gave me a knowing look, smiled and just walked away. And to myself I thought, "Oh well, just another day at the 1369 Café."

The Man on the Bench

*"Let me tell you someone's woe; storm clouds are on show;
But have no fear, the sun will someday reappear. I know that
life is not always fair, but it's always sunrise somewhere."
I was bouncing this ball in my hand and singing this song.
It's a little ditty I concocted to help keep my spirits up.*

It was just another ordinary cloudy day in Peabody Square when I first saw him. He came strutting into the park in his three piece suit, briefcase in hand and seemingly full of self importance; like he was the fucking Mayor or something. He sat right across from me and it was obvious that he didn't want to make eye contact with me. I kept staring him down though, if just to bug the hell out of him. So anyways, he had his head buried down in his book and I could tell that he was doing his best to pretend to be engrossed in it. And so I kept bouncing my ball and singing while staring him the fuck down. If just to bug the hell out of him. Guys like him get on my damn nerves. You know the type. They practically run this country: straight white males; full of delusional self-entitlement; usually wealthy, republican, suburban and their favorite pass time is looking down their noses at the rest of us while sucking on caviar and swigging champagne. As if God had set aside "special" rules just for them. As if they're some type of super human, not meant to receive the same blows life often throws at us little people. I'm more like him than he knew. As a matter of fact, I used to be him.

You see, I went to school with that douche bag; BU law to be exact. I have to admit; back then even *I* was a privileged white hetero full of myself and thinking that the goddamn world revolved around me. What a pretentious little piss as I was. Always sat in the front row. Always had an answer to every question the teacher threw at me. Hell, I was the teacher's pet. The teach always smiled profusely in my direction. I was such a looker back then, she couldn't help herself. From the way things looked, I wouldn't put it pass her to invite me over for some "private" tutoring had I needed it. But of course—being the cocky know it all that I was—I didn't. Heck even some of the male teachers couldn't help but stare at my male prowess over stuffed into my tight fitting jeans since I sat spread eagled in front of them; if just to exert my power over them. Yes, power can be a wonderful thing; that is, until that very power overpowers the one who possesses it.

I didn't mind their lascivious attention since I was and still am very secure in my masculinity. Anyways, I remember Mr. Designer suit from class. He was always striving to answer more questions than me, to get better grades than me, to come to class looking better than me. It was a sort of unspoken competition between us. I wouldn't put it pass him to want to measure our manhood's to see whose bigger. I'm sure I'd definitely win in that department. Anyways, after law school and a recommendation from my favorite teach, I got a job at a very prestigious law firm called Shuster & Shuster Law Inc. It was a father and son firm ubiquitous in the Boston area. I got my own apartment in the highly exclusive and expensive Newbury Street. I had a blond blue eyed girlfriend who was a doctor and was doing her residency at Boston Medical. We lived together and planned to have children within two years of our decision to cohabitate. Things couldn't be better. Life was so alive back then. The sun seemed to come out just for me; to take me to work in the morning and bring me back home in the evenings. Butterflies seemed to hover around my head and birds seemed to chirp esoteric songs only *I* was meant to hear and understand. My girl Lola was totally enamored with me and me with her. There were late summer days when I would lie on my back with my Lola on our roof deck, under the stars and the moon with the wondrous fascination and carefree spirit of children, both of us thinking that life can't possibly get any better than that moment and that God must be smiling down on us. But as with life, there are no guarantees and all good things eventually succumb to the often harsh realities of living. THINGS FALL APART!!!

One day, as I rose with the sun beaming against my window announcing a shiny silver morning, I felt a sudden surge of joy, anticipation and energy. Now mind you, I'm not a morning person; I don't usual succumb to over exuberance until at least noon time. So I thought the way I was feeling felt fairly peculiar to me. My energy level so high that my head began to spin around like a merry-go-round, I felt like leaves caught up in a wind infused upsweep of autumn; twirling around without a definite purpose and that was *before* I had my first cup of coffee. I got dressed and wolfed down my carnation instant breakfast, kissed my still sleeping Lola good bye and took off as if I was running from the devil. I remember racing down the highway and as trees and houses with white picket fences rushed passed me as I drove; my mind was racing right along with me. The sun was beating down so brightly, that I was starting to have trouble seeing, being that I wasn't wearing sunglasses, I started squinting. I also started to reflect about all the things I wanted to do with my life and regretting all the things that I haven't done yet. Then suddenly, as Scott Mc Kenszi's song "San Francisco" (if you're going to San Francisco/ be sure to wear some flowers in your hair) came on the radio, it occurred to me. I've always known that I'm a flower child at heart, despite my upper middle class upbringing. I'd always wanted to go on a trip across the vast lands of America. And so, in a mad haze of rocketing oomph and impulsivity, I decided to skip work and go on a cross country trip to San Francisco. Crazy? Yes. But reason and logic was not my conduit at that point. I wouldn't get an explanation for my sudden irrational behavior until much later. But until then, I just went along for the ride and this is my story.

In my mind, I woke-up—surprisingly perspicacious, acute and astute—to a hovering of blinding florescent lighting directly above me. I could hear a booming voice bust the otherwise halcyon setting, "I don't think he's going make it. He has simply lost too much blood from the impact of the accident." I figured then that I must be in a hospital, not heaven and the voice must be that of a doctor and not God; as I originally perceived. I wished so desperately that I could tell them that I was still alive. I tried to repel the tides of panic and pandemonium that was growing like a balloon inside of me, but it was no use. I wanted so much to shriek at the top of my lungs, "I'm alive! I'm alive! Please don't give up on me!" But all I could do was lie there, my fate completely out of my hands and I thought that this must be what helplessness really feels like.

I started to wonder how I had gotten there; to that point on an operating table; surrounded by men in white coats. The last thing I remembered was me driving down a high way. But where was I going? Why was I going there? Then all of a sudden I heard "Clear!" and then "We got him back!" Later, I found out that they went through my phone and contacted my wife Lola and told her what had happened. They then told her that I would have to be airlifted back to Boston since my car was impounded and that I was in San Francisco. San Francisco? I figured then that I must have been driving for days. They said I suffered from anterograde memory damage, which explains my inability to remember recent events.

When the ambulance brought me back home, Lola was waiting for me in front of the first floor window. I was so in love with her, not unlike Pygmalion, who in Greek mythology, fell in love with his self-made ivory statue and appealed to Aphrodite—Greek Goddess of love and beauty—to give it life, which she did. From a distance, she looked like a comely ghostly vision in a haunted mansion; fraught with trepidation, waiting to be rescued. Her eyes looked dark and hallow and her face was demure and seemingly expressionless. She was never one to show much emotion, perhaps it had to do with her profession as a doctor or having been raised by strict stoical German parents. She came running out to the ambulance as it pulled up to the house. The two EMT's helped me out and Lola ran into me to hug me and I almost lost my balance. "Easy, easy," I told her. She thanked the men and slowly walked me to the house. It was a cloudy autumn day and the fall leaves had resigned to their deaths on the ground in ample multiple mounts during my absence.

The house was immaculate, much like my Lola; even more so than usual. Lola cleans excessively under duress or when life is less than perfect. She sat me on the living room couch and tried to help me lie down, but I told her I was ok just to be sitting for now. And then, with a voice as gentle and earnest as a five year old child she asked me, "What happened?" I was dreading that question, because to tell you the truth, I don't really know what happened. And so I told her, "I don't remember. All I know is I woke up in a hospital and I was told that I was in a car accident and my head went through the windshield and that I was in coma for a while."

"Well, you left for work a week ago and you never returned I was worried sssick! But let's talk later. Right now, you need your rest." And she walked me to our bedroom and helped me to bed. Soon after, I fell into a deep sleep. And I began dreaming the most vivid dream I've ever dreamt.

I was in a deep green forest—the deepest green I'd ever seen—engulfed in purplish fog. And then there was this purple horse with long white elegant wings perched high in the air casually eating the vegetation. And then I realized that the white horse was me! Soon I began to fly around the forest, flapping my wings with graceful force, as the orange sun came down announcing the end of the day. Then I started to fly directly into the sunset until I was completely consumed by its rays.

The next thing I knew, I was being shaken awake by Lola announcing daybreak and the duty of breakfast. We just sat quietly eating together, as we usually do before we go off to work, even though I wasn't ready to return to work just yet. It's one of the ways we thought up to be with one another giving that both our work schedules tend to be very demanding and not at all friendly to the stability of our marriage.

Suddenly--an incongruity—Lola spoke and broke the spell; which startled me, because the only words that are usually spoken by either one of us at that particular moment are "love ya, have a nice day at work" conjoined with me giving her a butterfly kiss good bye.

"The doctors wrote down in your discharge papers that you talk to your primary care about possibly seeing aaaa...psy... chiatrist," she said with what appears to be an ingenuous but nervous smile while still looking down at her plate.

"Why would he do that? There's nothing wrong with me! Since when was speeding down the high way a psychological defect?" Lola was now looking up, her smile had dissipated and she could no longer hide the fear and concern in her eyes; she knows whenever I get so deliberately defensive, it usually means I know she's right and it's only a matter of time before I forfeit. She reached out and placed her supple porcelain like hands upon mines.

"Well, Carlton honey, just meet with him, see what he has to say. You must admit, what happened was somewhat mercurial and a little out of the ordi..."

"I DON'T want to talk about it!" Now highly irritated, I cut her off. "Let me just enjoy my breakfast in silence and we can talk about this later!"

"Well, would you rather that I dissemble?" She asked raising her eyebrows.

"Yes, doctor. I'd rather you dissemble. I want to *pretend* that everything is ok, at least for now. Can you do that for me, please?" I hardly ever snap at Lola and it scared me. What was happening to me? What was this "thing" inside of me causing me to act impulsively? It felt like in my head lurked a floating black and white TV, mysteriously showing an episode of... The Twilight Zone.

"Does he suspect anything?" asked Julian.

"No...no...at least I don't think so," Lola responded.

"How has he been since he was brought back from his impromptu trip to San Francisco?" Julian asked while staring at Lola with searching eyes. It was as if he wanted to hear bad news; something that would justify having an affair with his best friend's wife. He befriended Carlton while they were all attending BU together as undergrads. Julian, Lola and Carlton were known as The Inseparable Trio around campus. Julian was best man at Carlton's wedding. The fact that Lola and Julian were to do their internships at Boston Medical together elevated their relationship from mere platonic friendship and marked the onset of their burgeoning emotional intimacy leading to the actual affair.

"He seems to be getting increasingly worse. Just the other day, he woke up in the middle of the night screaming claiming that snakes were crawling all over him and then he went downstairs and plunged into our indoor pool fully clothed in an attempt to rid himself of them. I ended up having to stay up half the night holding him in my arms cradling and rocking him to sleep like a baby," Lola said with a wistful look in her eyes. And then suddenly she broke down in tears. "Oh, Julian. I don't know how much more of this I can take! I feel so guilty all the time. When I said for better or for worst in my marriage vows, I thought I meant them. But the stress has been overwhelming, so much so that I had to turn to you for moral support, not knowing that we would fall victim to immorality ourselves, what we're doing is wrong, just wrong..," "she leaned over and rested her head on Julian's shoulder as she continued to sob uncontrollably. They were in Julian's BMW which was parked in the parking lot of a local No Tell Motel.

"It's not your fault Carlton is coming undone and it's not wrong to seek support from a trusted family friend. I mean, don't get me wrong, Carlton is a great guy and I love him like a brother, however I didn't expect to fall in love with you, just like you didn't expect to fall in love with me. What happened happened and now, we have to be prepared to deal with the consequences, should we have to, "Julian had his right arm around Lola while looking straight ahead through the windshield as a triangle of birds flocked together in the orange haze of the late afternoon sun. He thought about what life would be like to feel that free; to look at the world from a bird's eye view; how big the world probably seem to them.

"Well, how long can we keep this up? How can I look him in the eye and tell him I love him when I know that it's no longer true. I care about him and I feel bad for what's happening to him but that's about it. I can't make my heart feel something it won't,"

Lola said as she remembered the Bonnie Rait song "I can't make you love me, if you don't." The winter air outside was tense and brisk. Through a partially opened window on Lola's side—which she had powered down because of her fear of suffocation in small enclosed places—she could hear the wind howling like the song of lonesome dog outside.

"You have to make him see a psychiatrist, "Julian said his eyes full of resolved determination.

"But he keeps saying that he's fine and he attributes his behavior to the stress he's been experiencing at the law firm," Lola said in an exasperated tone.

"Well, next time he behaves like a mad man, you have to take it upon yourself and call 911 and have him taken to the nearest psych ward. In case you haven't seen the news lately, mental illness left untreated can be lethal. Why, just the other day, I saw a news report about a manic depressive who stabbed his own mother with a knife during a fiery argument, killing her instantly. As it turned out, his mental illness was left untreated since the mad man refused to take his medication. Although In some cases, the medication itself has been known to cause violent behavior in the patient. Either way, next time he behaves like a mad man, you call 911 and have him committed, okay?" Julian's eyes were squinted, his eyebrows furrowed. Lola looked at him like a little girl being reprimanded by her father as she shook her head "yes" to his suggestion.

They then left the car and proceeded to go into the motel to be together. They stepped around a few remnants of tainted snow that had fallen the previous day and the low windows in the motel were partially stained with whitish snow blotches. Maybe it was because of everything that was going on—the guilt Lola felt, Carlton's mysterious illness and the fact that her marriage was unraveling—all compiled to make her desire for Julian that much more desperate and deliberate. Although she is not usually the aggressor, the minute the motel door was closed, Julian barely had enough time to turn around from hanging the Do Not Disturb sign and locking the door when Lola leaped onto his body, wrapping her arms and legs around him as if she was just pushed off a plane and he was her parachute and kissed him passionately. Julian, with his big hairy arms wrapped firmly around Lola, slowly stumbled around the room and unto the bed where he fell backwards with Lola landing on top of him all the while gasping for breath; as if they were trying to keep from drowning, having been caught in a tumultuous current of lust and forbidden desire. With his big perfectly manicured hands, he cupped her breasts; which hung like coconut sized orbs of dancing loveliness. They proceeded to practically tore off each other's clothes with a sense of urgent desperation and insatiable hunger.

At the moment of impact, Lola felt like a rocket launched inside of her as she cried out with unabated pleasure, her hands wrapped firmly around Julian's large and densely muscular body. The bed shook as if under seismic attack, the plaster cracked from behind the headboard banging violently against the wall and the partially opened champagne bottle did a jittery dance, crash landing onto the floor, it's foam slowly oozing and spreading at the exact moment they both cried out in unison, before Julian rolled off Lola, feeling as deflated as a popped balloon. They lay spent and grudgingly content as Julian lit up a cigarette that crackled and burned brightly in the darkness; while Lola had her head on his chest and her arms wrapped softly around his chiseled stomach. Soon, they got dressed to go back to the hospital to work through the night in the emergency room once again. As they were heading out the door, Julian looked at Lola and said, "Remember what I said, if it happens again you call…"

"911…I know," said Lola, with a slight hesitation in her voice. It was early evening, the street lights came on and so did the lights in the square house windows in the stillness of the night. Little did Julian and Lola knew that for one of them, the dark claws of death lurked in the shadows…

Beethoven's 5th symphony played violently in my head, with a demonic type of force and it made me floor the gas pedal. Everything in my peripheral vision was rushing by as if I was in a race car. I felt as though my soul was running on empty and soon, so will the car since I'd been too distracted to put gas in it. A sense of biting urgency was boiling within me; like I had very little time left; like a dying man whose cancer has metastasized throughout his entire body, leaving him minutes left to live. Speed! I felt the rush in my loins, my stomach, and my chest. I parked the car across from the motel and waited. Then, as the dark earth swallowed up the orange sun, I saw them. They were coming out of the motel with their arms around each other. Lola's head was partially resting on Julian's. They looked somber and somewhat pensive and I wonder if they felt any remorse for screwing me over by screwing each other. I watched them drive away and then I decided to go back to the house and wait for Lola to come home.

The house was unusually quiet when Lola came home from work. The moon that hovered over the house like a halo outside permeated throughout the entire house that glowed with a luminescent blue hue. So Lola didn't bother to turn on the lights, besides, being a nature lover, she welcomed the idea of the moon lighting up her abode. The only audible sounds were that of the vast variety of clocks ticking all over the house.

"Carlton?" She uttered, but no response was forthcoming. "Carlton honey, are you home?" Her voice began to crack a little with a modicum of warranted anxiety given Carlton's unpredictable behavior lately. She went to the bedroom to drop off her purse on the bed and her keys on the nightstand like she usually does. Then suddenly, the bedroom door slammed shut from behind her and there was Carlton, standing in front of it, wild eyed and snarling; like a lion engrossed in the brutal dance of predator and prey, with a long kitchen knife in his hand.

"So…how was *work*?" He said menacingly and sarcastically.

"It wasss…f-fine…Why-why do-do you look like that? And what are you doing with a knife?" Lola desperately tried to hide her fear but her voice shook anyways.

She remembered that she had the same fear when her father used to sneak into her room at night when she was just 5 years old. He used to crawl into bed with her and sang her lullabies and told her how much he loved her; told her that he was just expressing his love for her when he touched her in places that she was shy about; telling her that if she ever told anyone, that she would be sent away and never see mommy and daddy again. How his behavior continued well into her teens until one day she found the courage to fight him off; she was so angry that she took a knife and tried to castrate him while he slept, but just ended up wounding him as he desperately fought her off. She was angry at her mother for not noticing the signs and for thinking that it was somehow her fault when she finally found out; she had lived with this secret that had caused her shyness. Now, the knife was in someone else's hand and she could not help but think that this was her nemesis for what she tried to do to her dad.

She married Carlton because she thought that she was damaged goods and that had she not said yes to his proposal, that no one else would want her. She often felt like she was wearing a huge sign on her that announced her secret shame to the entire world and Carlton was the only one who did not see it. After all, she was the daughter of well mannered, well to do parents, so of course she felt that no one would ever believe her had she spoke of her shame earlier. So now, with Carlton on the brink of madness, she had decided not to keep anymore secrets; she decided to confide in Julian.

"I saw you! I saw you *with* him!" Being full of rage, Carlton's voice was raising much like the blood that had welled up in his eyes.

"You saw me with whom?" Lola pretended not to know what he was talking about, if only to buy herself sometime.

"Don't play dumb with me. You always did make a lousy liar. I saw you with Julian at that sleazy motel. I eavesdropped on a conversation you two were having once while you thought I was sleeping. You were making plans with that sonofabitch in my fucking house! It was soon after I was brought back from San Francisco." Carlton looked like a man who had just swallowed a bottle of hot sauce; his eyes full of fire and fury. Lola was slowly backing away so not to inveigle his rage any further. "Carlton, now...put the knife away, we can talk about this..." She said pleadingly.

"Oh...*now* you wanna talk, eh? Don't you think it's a bit too late for that? Perhaps it would have been better to talk *before* you decided to fuck my best friend!" Carlton looked completely unreasonable by now and it quickly became obvious to Lola that he had made up his mind about whatever his intentions were; which left Lola feeling like a trapped animal. "Get on the bed and on your stomach...now!" He commanded and she reluctantly obliged. He then walked over and straddled her. He grasped both of her hands then pulled a rope out of his pocket and proceeded to tie her up. Meanwhile, Lola's phone began to ring unrelentingly. "That's probably your boyfriend calling...I'm gonna make sure that you two never get the chance to make a fool out of me again!" Carlton barked, practically foaming at the mouth by this point. He turned Lola over, ripped up her blouse, lifted her skirt, yanked off her lace panties and began raping her. When she began to scream, he stuffed her underwear into her mouth and she bit him. "You bitch!" He said as he slapped her. As she wiggled from under him, her eyes widened in horror as she watched him reach for the knife. "You're gonna pay now. No one makes a fool out of me and gets away with it, "He said as sweat poured from his reddened face. "You see what you're making me do. Why did you have to do it? Why?" He cried out like an trapped animal in agony. And just as he raised the knife aimed directly at her heart, a voice startled him. "Carlton! You don't wanna do this! Please put the knife down!"

Julian had decided to come over worried—and with the angels of good fortune on his side—found the front door unlocked since Lola and Carlton seldom locked their doors. At the sound of Julian's voice, Carlton bounded off the bed and launched at Julian but he backed up swiftly, just missing the sting of the blade. "You sonofabitch, you're fucking my wife!" Carlton got into a semi-crouching position and launched for Julian once again and this time, he sliced his shoulder blade but Julian managed to knock the knife out of his hand and the two men began wrestling on the floor. Carlton had Julian in a choke hold and had managed to slide over to where the knife was and by the time he reached it and was primed to stab Julian right in the chest, Lola's voice yelped from behind him, "Drop the knife Carlton! Don't make me have to use this!" Lola had wiggled herself free and was now pointing the gun she had bought and hid under the mattress when Carlton began to act erratically. Something that Julian suggested that she does just in case he became violent. Carlton, having been startled briefly turned around, allowing Julian to quickly free himself from under him. Julian stood just as Carlton went after Lola, knife in hand and screaming "You're gonna get it now bitch!" Lola fired the gun and to her surprise, it was Julian who fell to the ground clutching his chest. She started screaming and Carlton, panicked and scared, fled the scene while Lola frantically dialed 911.

***

A few days after the incident, Carlton was found wondering the streets looking disheveled and spouting gibberish and was incarcerated in a jail for the criminally insane until he was released to the streets five years later. Lola was jailed for manslaughter for killing Julian. Having lost everything, Carlton found himself spending most of his days sleeping on park benches waiting for his lost life to come back and rescue him.

It's Always Sunrise Somewhere

The alarm clock is buzzing 6 a.m. and Hank Harrington is rustling in bed fighting the urge to roll over and go back to sleep. It is yet another cloudy day in Peabody and Hank—a victim of the floundering economy—is dreading yet another day of pretending to go to work at the law firm. His wife Wilma and his twin boys Justin and Jason have no idea that their privileged lives are about to change.

Hank grew up in an upper middle class family in Peabody, Massachusetts. His father was a doctor and had a home based medical practice and his mother was a housewife. Hank, being an only child, always acquired whatever his spoiled heart desired. But his world was turned upside down when his mom became dissatisfied with being a housewife and wanted to go to Hollywood in hopes of becoming a movie star. Their marriage was coming undone during the late sixties, at the cusp of the woman's liberation movement. Hank's mom decided to divorce his dad, leaving Hank behind and went on an impulsive trip to Hollywood in pursuant of her dreams. Hank resolved then to pursue his *own* dreams of becoming a civil rights lawyer.

Hank ended up going away to college at Boston University where he did both his undergraduate and graduate work. It was there he met Wilma. After graduation, they soon married and moved back to his childhood home to take care of his ailing dad. After his dad died, the house of course was left to Hank. Soon, they settled down and a year later the boys were born. Wilma, who also studied law, decided to stay at home to raise the boys since Hank worked at one of the most prestigious law firms in Boston and was well on his way of making partner.

As the sun tries desperately to break through the silver clouds, he goes for his usual morning jog before feigning going to work.

As he runs through the deep woods contiguous to his house, his thoughts start to jog along with him. He remembers the lavish life style his dad used to live. He would buy a new car every time their next door neighbors bought one, He would take them on expensive vacations, buy fur coats and jewelry constantly for Hanks' mom and buy anything Hank asked for. What Hank and his mom did not know was that his dad had a gambling problem and was entombed in debt. So like most Americans, he was living beyond his means. Hank remembers thinking that he did not want that to happen to him and his family. He tried to be particularly careful with his spending and for the most part was successful. However—as he jogs through the intricate pathways of the woods and as low hanging tree branches slaps him in his face—he never predicted that one day he would be out of a job. He thinks that America has lied to him: work hard and you can live the American Dream…"Yeah…right," he says out loud.

He kisses Wilma and the boys' good bye after breakfast before leaving; his destination: the park in Peabody Sq. When he gets there, he looks up to see the sun still hiding behind the silver clouds and the pigeons are flocking to whoever is willing to feed them, even though there are signs posted that say, "Don't feed the pigeons." He starts thinking about how he's going to provide for his family. He looks up to see a yellow autumn leaf fall from an adjacent tree as if in slow motion. Hank follows it down with his eyes until it hits the ground without making a sound. He wonders what it would feel like to be this light. People with somewhere to be are hustling and bustling all around him. He puts his briefcase down and sits on a bench and he notices a man—who appears to be homeless—sitting across from him. Suddenly he feels a flood of fear welling up in him, and he thinks that if he doesn't do something, it would drown him. So he tries to block the man out of his sight by looking left and right or down at his open book to avoid making eye contact with him. But the man kept staring right at Hank all the while bouncing a ball in his right hand. He could feel the man's eyes peering through him as if he recognizes Hank and is just waiting for Hank to recognize *him.*

But Hank methodically keeps his eyes transfixed on his book, even though he really isn't reading at all. Suddenly this eerie feeling begins to permeate throughout his body. A sense of déjà vu swiveled around in his head. *Who is this man?* He was thinking to himself: *why is this homeless looser staring at me? Perhaps he wants to rob me. As he can see based on the way I look with my three piece suit that I'm above him in every way possible. I maybe out of a job, but I'm still a BU grad with a law degree and am in anyway like that disheveled looking bum on the bench.*

Then suddenly he looks up and his eyes squint with furrowed brows as he looks across at the man. He can feel his heart accelerating and he begins to breathe short agitated breaths from his chest up. The man is still staring at him, unflinching and starts singing this song: "Let me tell you what I know, storm clouds are gonna blow. But have no fear, the sun will someday reappear. I know that life is not always fair, but it's always *sunrise somewhere*." And then he repeats the song all over again while still bouncing the ball and scrutinizing Hank.

Hank can feel an intense unexplainable feeling of hatred for the man; looking across at him, he thinks about how he resents this stranger; how unkempt he looks; how red his white face is; how filthy his finger nails are. But there is something about the man's eyes that is almost completely separate from the rest of his body. The man's eyes seem to twinkle in spite of how pallid the rest of his face looks. For some reason, that makes Hank even angrier.

Hank then gets up and strides over to him, now towering over him and basically barks at him, "What the fuck you're looking at? What, you after my wallet or something? You waiting for me to dose off so you could steal my sixteen hundred dollar alligator shoes? I'm not like you! I have a family, I drive a Mercedes and have a beautiful home in an exclusive neighborhood. What have *you* got besides the clothes on your back and criminal intents in your head? So stop fucking staring at me like you know me or something cause you clearly don't, got it?" At this point he was shaking with emotion. And as he begins to walk away, the man—who never stopped bouncing his ball—simply continues singing: "Let me tell someone's woe, storm clouds are on show. But have no fear, the sun will someday reappear. I know that life is not always fair, but it's always *sunrise somewhere.*"

As Hank starts to walk around the city, still shaken from his recent encounter with the man on the bench, a wave of realization begins to creep up on him. *I remember! I remember!* He thinks to himself. He realizes where he has seen the guy before. It was while he was attending law school at BU. He remembers him being a very charismatic man who always sat in the front of the class. He wonders what happened to him. How could he go from being a promising law student to being a dirty man on a park bench? And the fear he felt when he sat across from the man begins to subside. He can feel sprinkles of water dripping down on his blue suit and he wonders if it had started raining; that is until he realizes that it is his own tears cascading down his sullen face.

His steps abruptly become much slower and methodical. Should he just come clean and confess to his family that their way of life is in jeopardy? He reaches an intersection and all the lights were a steady red and the signs are flashing "Stop". He then decides to go home early and begins to walk with light excited steps. He looks up in the sky to see the sun finally emerging and shining down on him and he smiles knowingly. He then suddenly stops walking and—with a smile and eyes wide open—tilts his head back to feel the sun blanketing his face.

Printed in the United States
By Bookmasters